Oh, Brother!

GE

Oh, Brother!

by Corinne Gerson

Atheneum 1982 New York

LIBRARY OF CONGRESS CATALOGING IN PUBLICATION DATA

Gerson, Corinne.
Oh, brother.

SEQUEL to: Son for a day.
SUMMARY: Danny establishes himself as the favorite adopted kid brother for four Chicago teenage boys who in turn inspire him to become a Renaissance Man.
[1. Friendship—Fiction] I. Title.
PZ7.G3220h [Fic] 81-8052
ISBN 0-689-30878-7 AACR2

Published simultaneously in Canada by
McClelland & Stewart, Ltd.
Composed by American–Stratford Graphic Services, Inc.
Brattleboro, Vermont
Manufactured by Fairfield Graphics
Fairfield, Pennsylvania
First Edition

TO ROGER:
Son for every day,
Who made this book possible

AND BRUCE:
The Big Brother

Oh, Brother!

Chapter 1

I never thought a kid who grew up in New York City would ever want to live anywhere else. But when my ma got this terrific job in Chicago and we moved out there, I really liked it. We got a neat apartment in a little building near the University, with nice big rooms and trees and grass outside.

It didn't take me long to find one of the greatest places for kids in all of Chicago. And it was close enough to my house to walk to. This guy Steve took me there my very first Saturday in Chicago. His ma and mine met at work, and you know how mothers are: the next thing I knew, I had a friend that I didn't even know if I wanted. But it turned out okay, because he asked me would I like to go to this special museum where they had all kinds of exhibits you could fool around with yourself and it was a whole lot of fun. Now, I was never much for museums. I personally like action and people. Well, I sure had a great big surprise waiting for me at the Museum of Science and Industry. As dead as it sounds, I never dreamed there was a place like that, and I never saw so much action.

That first time I went there with Steve was one

of the most exciting days of my whole entire life, for two reasons. First, the place itself had the kind of stuff I always dreamed about—the real, actual Apollo space capsule, all opened up so you can see inside it and how the astronauts had to lie down to keep attached. Right when you walk in there's an F-104 Starfighter—a phantom jet—hanging from the ceiling. A *real* one! It's so much smaller than you'd expect. And they have all these exhibits with computers that you can work yourself to get information from and even play games with. With all the terrific attractions in New York, it doesn't have anything like that.

Then, the second reason it was so great: I had this MO in New York—that's like a game plan—where I found myself a whole bunch of fathers and sons that I'd picked up at the Bronx Zoo when they came there to spend visiting day with each other. See, a lot of divorced men have to take their kids out one day a weekend, and they often end up at the zoo looking a little lost and—you know—sort of uneasy. It got so I could spot them, and I'd just ease into a friendly conversation, and before you knew it, I was invited to lunch and then to whatever else they were doing for the rest of the day. I got to go all over the New York area, and there's hardly anything there I didn't do or see—and all for free! It got so I had so many "families" I had to mark down appointments in a datebook. My zoodaddies were so great it was better than having your own father, which I don't have, because you can pick them yourself. And the kids—they were better than having your own little brothers: you never even had the chance to fight with them.

But life got too good. I goofed up the whole thing by telling my story to a nice woman who turned out to be a TV star, and she was so fascinated by it she blabbed it all on her show and blew my cover. Oh, she didn't mean to; she didn't even say who I was, but it all leaked out, and I got to be some celebrity! I even ended up on TV myself, and my ma, too. That's how she got this good job in Chicago, which is why we moved here.

Well, you can imagine what I thought when I first went to that museum that Saturday with Steve. It was mobbed, like it always is on weekends, and my trained eye saw all these men holding the hands of little kids, and I thought, *Wow, a whole new territory!* What better way to take in Chicago than with museumdaddies. I started the whole ball rolling the very next weekend. And first time out, it rolled into a ditch.

I still don't know if it was because I fell into the hands of people like the Peabodys, or if it was the other thing: that I was outgrowing zoodaddies and museumdaddies and any kind of daddies. Because I was twelve by now, and with just one shot at my old MO in new clothing, I had lost my touch.

Steve had told me the coal mine was about the neatest exhibit at the museum, but the line to get in was too long the day we were there. I went to look the place over that second weekend—there was a line again, but it wasn't very long. You had to pay for the tour, though, and I only had a quarter, so I figured I'd see it some other time.

"We're going in a *real coal mine,*" this twirpy kid said to me as I passed by. He had blond curly hair and weasely blue eyes and a funny, crooked smile. He was little and fat—eight or nine, I guessed.

"Yeah, that's nice," I said. "You're lucky."

The man with him was wearing a funky jacket and a real friendly smile. "Ever been on this tour?" he asked me.

"No, but I will sometime. There are real coal-mine cars and they take you down into the exact replica of a mine." How about that *replica.* I got it from the museum booklet I picked up when I went with Steve.

"Is that right?" the man said, giving me this shrewd look that I knew all about. Yep, sure enough he looked down at little squirt, sizing up the whole situation—me, and him, and them.

"OOOOh, I can't wait!" little squirt squeaked. He could have been Donald or even Bobby, or any of the "little brothers" I had "adopted" in New York. He turned out to be Charles. Not Charlie. Not Chuck. *Charles.*

"Be patient, Charles, we'll be going in any minute." A nice, fatherly smile. I wasn't certain about this dude—about whether he'd measure up to go into my datebook. I was certain enough what his next words would be, though: "Uh, would you like to come along with us, son?"

Son. Well, that could be good; it could be bad. We'd see how lunch went.

Charles was crazy about the coal mine; and he was crazy about the Money Center and the Hall of Communications where you can play Tic-Tac-Toe on the computers. Of course, he was crazy about me. "Hey, Dad, can Danny come with us for lunch?"

Dad. This eight-year-old squirt called his father Dad. I sort of scrunched up my mouth to keep from laughing. He was a pretty funny kid, with tight little curls and a loud squeaky voice. Old Dad sounded like honey spilling out of a jar and looked down at you from under these icy blue eyes with fat lids. I decided I'd keep a low profile all through lunch, which of course I got invited to, and which of course I very humbly accepted. Then I would see what was what with this pair. But I never even made it that far.

An icy wind whipped at us the moment we stepped outside. It was only the middle of October, the time when you could still wear a lightweight jacket in New York; but one thing I found out about Chicago right away was you have to like being cold to live there: winter comes early. I put my head down as we walked into the wind in the museum parking lot, where their car was parked.

It was a long-nosed, low-to-the-ground foreign sports job, a two-seater. Squirt and I shared the passenger seat, and he started getting a great big kick out of elbowing me in the gut every time he said something he thought was funny, which was about every two minutes. I'd try to move away, but there wasn't any place to move. We were driving a pretty long while, and none of the things he said were even funny. I was getting pretty sore and finally said, "Hey, Charles, that hurts—cut it out!"

"Yeah?" said he and then gave me a real big one. So I just wound up and gave him a big one right back, right in his little pot belly. You never heard such a yell. Mr. Peabody swerved the car, and Charles kept yelling and carrying on and telling his father I'd punched him. Old Dad pulled over to the corner, calmly reached over past me, opened the door, and said, hardly opening his mouth: "Out."

I looked at him kind of blank. I had no idea where I was. We had been driving in and out of a lot of streets, and by now I didn't have the faintest notion of which way we'd gone. All I knew was it didn't look like anywhere I'd ever been in my life.

"Okay," I said, "but, uh, where—"

"Just get out," Mr. Peabody growled now, his lips curled against his teeth. I got out. As the car streaked away, I could still hear Charles yowling.

I put my hands in my pockets and felt my door key, a quarter, and a stick of gum. Period. I looked around and saw all kinds of stores. I started thinking about going into one to try to find out how I could get back home when a police car pulled up and stopped for the light. Painted in nice big letters along the side was, "We Serve and Protect." I walked over.

"Excuse me—can you tell me how to get to the Museum of Science and Industry?"

The driver was an older guy, the fatherly type. The other one was young with a big mustache. "Yeah, well," The Mustache began, "you go down—oh, about eight blocks, till you get to—" He stopped suddenly and kind of screwed up his eyes at me. "You planning to walk there, or what?"

"Well, I only have a quarter, so, yeah, I guess I have to walk. Is it far?"

He turned to his partner, who nodded, then turned back to me as he reached to open the back door. "Hop in, kid, we're going right past it."

Boy, it sure was great to get out of the wind and cold, into that nice, warm car. But I was disappointed that it didn't have grilles on the windows and special locks and stuff—it was just like a regular car on the inside.

"Where do you live, fella?" The Mustache was turning, smiling at me. When I told him my address, he laughed. "Bet you haven't lived there long. From New York, hey?"

I was amazed. "How did you know?"

The driver hooted. "With that accent, it takes about two seconds to figure it out."

"Well, I only came out here two weeks ago. Give me time, I might even be talking like you guys!" I didn't have the nerve to add: "Through your noses."

The Mustache gave me a sharp look, but when he saw my grin he laughed along with the driver, who said now, "Hey, kid, are you really going to the museum?" I saw them exchange a funny look.

I hunched down in the seat a little. All of a sudden those uniforms looked scary. All of a sudden I was sorry for being such a wiseguy. "Well, as a matter of fact, I got myself a little lost, but I know my way home from there, so—"

"So maybe we'll just give you a free ride and make sure you get to the right place. What number did you say that was?"

When they got to my building, The Mustache got out, opened my door, and nodded to his partner. "Okay, let's get you back to your teddy bear. Where to?" He was looking down at me a little impatiently, and I felt all mixed-up.

"What do you mean? This"—and I nodded at the building we were standing in front of—"is where I live."

"Okay, fine. That's what you said before. Now let's get you into the right cubbyhole, okay?" He took my arm, and I couldn't decide whether I was proud or ashamed: he was going to take me right into my apartment!

When my ma opened the door I forgot about pride and shame because she turned all white and I thought she was going to faint.

"Danny, what's wrong?"

"Nothing, ma'am, he's fine—just got lost so we're delivering him to you."

"REALLY?" My ma stared at him, then at me, then burst into one of her big smiles. "Oh, Officer, thank you! Danny, where did you get lost? I thought you were down at the museum."

"I was, but—I'll tell you all about it, M
a long story. Thanks a lot for the ride, Officer.
was real nice of you."

He gave a little salute and a big smile. "Se
you around, buddy."

I hated to see him go. My ma was standing there looking at me, and I couldn't put it off any longer: I had to tell her how I got lost.

"I can't believe it!" she shrieked when I finished my story. "I thought you put all that behind you, Danny, in New York. I thought the zoodaddies were a thing of the past. Oh, honey," and her face crumpled the way it did when she was about to cry.

"I did, Ma, I did. *Honest!*" I grabbed her hand. "Listen, this is the truth. I couldn't help myself. I was standing there at the coal mine exhibit, all by myself, and then there was this man and his squirty kid gawking and yapping about how they wondered this and they wondered that, and I'd read all about it because—*you* know, I was really interested in it. So I just naturally started answering their questions, the way any normal human being would, and the next thing I knew, they were asking me to go see it with them—"

"And of course you couldn't refuse because you knew you'd love it so much—"

"Yeah. How did you know?"

My ma was grinning now. "Besides, it was so nice having company. Much better than seeing it all by yourself."

"Yeah. You know how it is, Ma."

"And they loved having you along. It was hard to tell who liked it more, the father or the kid—"

"How did you know?"

She was giggling now. "So then they invited you to come have lunch with them."

I was nodding, laughing with her now.

"And maybe even to—let's see, is the circus in town? Or something like that?"

"Well, it never got that far." The laughing kind of echoed in my ears in a funny way now. "See, what happened was . . ." I looked across the room and parked my stare on her funny little needlepoint picture as I stumbled through the terrible scene with the Peabodys. I didn't look up till I got to the part about the police car, and when I did, Ma's big blue eyes were misted over.

"What terrible people they are!" She reached over and hugged me, and I wanted to faint from her perfume.

"Hey, Ma, take it easy!"

She burst out laughing. "Did anyone ever tell you you're a funny little bugger?" She got stern again. "Now look, Danny, we're going to have to have a real understanding about this whole thing."

I put up my hands. "Listen, Ma, I promise you I'm never going to do it again. Honest. Ma, I know you won't believe me when I tell you this, but—will you try?"

She raised her hand with the Girl Scouts honor sign.

"Well, all the way home in that police car I was

thinking. Real hard. I thought about all those great times I had in New York, at the zoo, and the terrific things I did and saw, and it was only natural for me to try to run the same old MO right here in Chicago. I mean, don't get me wrong, I wasn't planning it beforehand, honest I wasn't. It just sort of happened, like a—a *reflex,* when I set foot in that museum. But such a funny thing—this one trip out with the Peabodys, and I'm *cured!*"

Her blue eyes were wide with trust. "But how do you know, Danny? How can you be so sure?"

"Ma, I knew something was different when we were walking out to their car. I mean, there was no reason to be suspicious of them or anything—they were being real nice and friendly and it was all going on so smooth, the way things always did. But there was a thing that was really, really different about it all."

"What, Danny? What was it?"

"I didn't know what it was then, but I looked at this guy and this squirty kid and I had these funny feelings about them. Not like in New York when I used to look at them and wish—well, you know—that I sort of belonged to their little family. This time I felt kind of *bored.* I almost wished I could get it over with so I could come home and . . ." I shrugged, feeling all mixed-up.

"But I don't understand." Ma's brow was wrinkled. "If you felt that way, why were you going with them? Why—"

"That's what I asked myself!" I cried. "And I

didn't know the answer. Not till I came home. Hey, those cops were real nice to me, bringing me home, and all that, but I knew it was because they thought I was a runaway and they wanted to make sure. You know what? They spotted my New York accent!"

"I always heard Chicago cops are smart." She was smiling again. "Oh, Danny, you can't imagine how I felt when I opened the door and saw you standing there with that policeman."

"I know, Ma, but listen. That's when it hit me. I don't need them any more."

"I know, honey—they brought you home safe, and you won't need them again, let's hope."

"No, I don't mean that. I mean the zoodaddies. Or the museumdaddies. Or *any* daddies. Not even police daddies. I've grown out of that, Ma. So you don't have to worry anymore. It's never going to happen again." I put my hand over my heart. "I promise."

That was when we decided to celebrate. "Tomorrow is going to be a special all-day celebration," Ma announced. "Starting with breakfast, which, since it's Sunday, will be in bed."

"In *bed!* I don't want to eat breakfast in bed—I hate crumbs in my sheets."

"Who said anything about *you?*" She had this silly smirk. "For *me*. In *my* bed. You will serve it to me there, whatever you decide to make. And"—she gave me a little shove—"it has to be more than toast. And real coffee, not instant."

"Aw, Ma—"

"Isn't that all right, Danny?" No one in the world had a sweeter smile than my ma. "I mean, it *is* a celebration."

"Yes, but it sounds like I'm doing all the work so far and you're doing all the celebrating."

She frowned now. "That's true. But you didn't hear the rest. Afterwards you're taking me to a very special place."

"Me taking you?" That was my ma all right. I knew she had something pretty special planned for us. I tried to think of what the best thing was you could do in Chicago.

"Yes, Danny. You're going to take me to the Museum of Science and Industry. I want to see all those wonderful things you've been telling me about —the coal mine and the computers you can play around with and the submarine and the space capsule . . ."

I stared at her, blinking to make sure I was seeing and hearing right. I was. She looked like a little kid just told she was going to take a tour of a candy factory, with free samples.

"And I promise you, Danny, we won't pick up any museumdaddies."

We didn't. We picked up a teenager instead. And that was the beginning of a whole new MO. *His*. But we didn't know that then.

Chapter 2

I'd rather skip the breakfast part of that next day, because it was too gruesome. Listen, I really tried. I thought the whole thing was pretty dumb, but I knew it would make my ma happy so I brought her apple juice in a champagne glass—she loved that—and scrambled eggs that were hard, beady little things and coffee that smelled like burned-out tires. She's a good sport, though, my ma—she sat up in bed against a whole bunch of pillows in a blue fluffy robe that matched her eyes and said she felt like a queen and that one of these days I'd learn to be a good cook. I found out later you have to put more than a pat of butter in the skillet when you make scrambled eggs, and who knows what went wrong with the coffee. I had to leave the frying pan in the sink to soak for a couple days.

"This is the best toast I ever had," she said, arranging those rubbery little pieces of egg on her second slice. I poured myself another glass of milk to wash down the rest of the fluffernutter that was my breakfast treat. She kept looking at it in a strange way, and I had the funny feeling she'd have rather had my breakfast. But none of that mattered once we got going. It didn't even matter that it was gray and rainy out, because there was something crackly in the air. That was what my ma always said: "When there's something crackly in the air, you can tell it's going to be a special day." I can't explain just what that means, the same way she never could explain it to me when I was little, but I grew to understand it the way she did, and knew it was true. And sure enough, that day was special.

My ma flipped for the museum. The neat thing about it is that even though it's for kids, the grown-ups who come with them have as much fun. Sometimes more. See, they have the chance to show the kids how to do this and that and explain everything just because they're parents. But the truth is, the kids don't need to be shown or explained to, they can figure out most things for themselves. In a way I guess you could say it's a great place for kids to take their parents to. It sure was true for my ma. Her eyes just about bugged out from the minute we walked in and she saw that phantom jet hanging from the ceiling and found out it was real, one that was used in World War II.

"Look," she said then, pointing across the lobby floor, "Food for Life. Let's go see that, okay?"

I shrugged and followed along. It was her trip. I couldn't imagine how she could face even the idea of food after that breakfast, but there we were, planted in front of a moving display of cereal, fruit, and yes—even eggs!

"You do it, Danny," she said, pointing at the

computer as she read the instructions to me. All of a sudden she looked like all the other parents draped over the little computers with their kids, explaining things to them. "Here, now you have to punch in your age and sex and weight—do you know how much you weigh, Danny?—and you get a number—"

"Yeah, yeah, I know." I'd done some of this when I was there the first time, with Steve, but not very much because it was real crowded then, too, and we didn't get a chance at that many computers. Now when I got my number, I asked her to help pick out the menu. Then it would give me all kinds of information about the food value I was getting. I tried to choose my favorite foods, like hamburgers and pizza, and she kept telling me to change it to stuff she thought was better. It took us so long to finish my menu that the computer erased the whole thing and started over, so I just pulled my ma over to the next exhibit: a bicycle that's supposed to show on a scale of one to eight how much energy you can work up when you pedal it. My ma hopped on and pedaled away like crazy, but she couldn't get it past four. The harder she tried, the more I cracked up, and she got real mad and said if I was so great let's see what I could do. That it had to be broken, and I'd find out soon enough.

I got on the way I get on a bike, without even sitting on the seat, and then decided just to keep on doing it like that, standing up on the pedals, and I got it up to seven! My ma put her hands on her hips and shook her head the way she does when she's annoyed, but then she burst out laughing.

"You know why it's so hard, don't you?"

We both turned around and saw this teenager watching us. He was a tall stringbean of a guy with dark hair, acne, and a shy smile. There was something about him that reminded me of someone I knew, but I couldn't figure out who. Not till much later.

"Yeah, well . . ." I began, and my ma asked eagerly, "No, why? I thought it was broken."

"Oh, no, it's meant to be that way. I don't know why, because it's supposed to measure the energy you expend on the basis of pedaling the bicycle. But instead of how hard you pedal, it really measures how *fast* you pedal. And it's really hard to do it fast because the pedals don't have any resistance."

"Oh-h-h," says my ma, "then it's *supposed* to be hard like that. I only did four." She smiled sheepishly.

He grinned at her. "That's very good for someone your size."

"It is?" She started looking proud.

"Sure. And *you*—" He was studying me now. He had nice gray eyes. "Seven is fantastic!"

I just smiled back at him and shrugged.

"Of course," he went on, "you beat the system. You stood on the pedals. You can go a lot faster that way. It's the speed that did it, not the energy." He laughed a croaky laugh then and pushed my shoulder back with his big paw, the way pals do to each other. "You're a pretty smart little operator, aren't you! Hey, how old are you, anyway?"

"Twelve."

He shook his head and gave a funny whistle. "Well, you sure have lots of energy, anyway."

"How old are you?" my ma asked him.

"Sixteen."

She looked around now. "Did you come with a little brother or sister?"

He dropped his eyes. "Well, not exactly. I mean, I just thought I'd drop in, I was going by and all—"

"Oh, I don't blame you!" she cried. "This looks like one of the greatest places in the world. If Danny hadn't brought me here, I'd never have known about it."

He grinned at her now, pointing just across the aisle with his chin. "How'd you like the baby chicks?"

"We haven't seen them yet," she replied. "We just got here."

"Oh, then you'll want to see them getting hatched. They ought to be ready soon."

Her eyes grew big and round. *"Really?* Right before our *eyes?"*

"If you're lucky. I was over there before, but nothing much was happening. At least, nothing we could see. But those little critters are inside there pecking away, you can bet on it, because they always put them in the display incubator on hatching day." I just kept staring at him. He seemed to know about *everything* here. *Who did he remind me of?* "Want to come over with me and check?"

My ma really went bonkers when she saw this teeny, fuzzy chick stalking around on wobbly little legs and an eggshell standing right there that he had busted out of. "That must've come out just before I got here the first time," our new friend was saying, "because he is just standing there exhausted. It takes a while till they start moving around. After all, they've been pecking at the shell for practically a whole day. It's the hardest work they ever do in their lives."

"My goodness," says my ma now, looking at him with admiration, "how do you know so much about this? About everything they have here? Do you come here a lot?"

Now I knew who he reminded me of.

He shrugged. "I used to, when I was little. I still stop by just to check things out." Now *he* grinned sheepishly. "I like to read up on stuff. I just love facts. Eat 'em up."

"Well, isn't that—isn't that *interesting,*" my ma said, then looked at me. "See, Danny—oh," and then she turned back to him, "this is Danny Turner, my son, and you are—?"

"I'm Raymond Rafferty. Pleased to meet you, Ms. Turner," He bobbed his head at her politely, then stuck his hand out to me. "Danny?"

I shook it. He had a firm grip. I heard that means you have a good character. "Hi," I said.

"Oooh, look!" my ma cried then, waving at one of the eggs as a pointy little thing stuck through.

"That's the egg tooth!" Raymond cried. There

was a whole big crowd around, and everyone was buzzing with excitement. "Look, look, there's the beak!" Raymond said. My ma was actually gasping, and my eyes were just about falling out of my head as all of a sudden this little bugger came busting through his shell, all wet and with tiny pieces of shell stuck to him in different places. Kids and grown-ups were screeching all over the place; and when it just lay all still, I was sure it was dead but I didn't dare say it.

"It's dead!" one little kid wailed, and Raymond turned to her, saying, "No, no, it's only recovering from all that hard work. Just wait, you'll see, it'll be walking around in a little while."

He was right. We watched as it got itself up on its shaky little legs, got all dried off and fluffed up, and then started hobbling around. My ma was glued to the display case. After it had stalked around to the other side, she turned to us with this rapt expression. "This was one of the most special experiences of my life. I will never eat eggs again." Then, turning to Raymond: "Do they have a restaurant in this place?"

He nodded. "A few of them."

"Will you come and have lunch with us?"

"Oh, that's really nice of you, but—"

"Please," she said, "we really want you to. Don't we, Danny?"

I shrugged and smiled. "Sure. Come on, Raymond."

We had hamburgers and French fries and

laughed about what nutritional value they would show on the computer. And after that, we did another two hours of the museum, the three of us. I couldn't remember when I had enjoyed myself so much.

Raymond took us to some of his favorite exhibits, and to others he thought my ma would get a special kick out of, like the Fairy Castle and the Circus. Our hands-down favorite, my ma and me, was the Vintage Car of the Future, which runs on boiled shaving lotion and has a barbecue in the back and a harp and all kinds of hilarious things that this funny guy with a fancy British accent tells you about when you listen on the earphones. We stood there lined up listening and laughing our heads off, while Raymond went over to examine the Tension Tower, his favorite. "One of these days," he said, "I'm going to figure out how it can stay up like that, without any apparent supports." Me, I can't even describe it! We loved the electronic painting, too, and the fascinating displays of optical illusions with colored lights. My ma wanted to see things like the Petroleum Exhibit—because the moving chairs that go through it, in their little shells with telephones that you listen in to, looked like fun—but Raymond said, "No, you don't want to waste your time on that—it's just a lot of propaganda hogwash. You'll like the Mathematica exhibit much better."

He was right again. Of course, me and my ma didn't exactly know which end was up between Celestial Mechanics and Projective Geometry and Probability Boards, but Raymond explained them so well we really understood the general ideas behind them. I got a kick out of the way he talked like an encyclopedia, and I kept thinking, boy, he sure is smart—I wonder if I could ever be smart like that! Maybe if I stuck around him a lot I could be. Besides, I really liked him. He was real friendly and down-to-earth, but he wasn't fresh or pushy. And he kept being really interested in things I said and things I asked him. So when it was time to go and my ma invited him home for our Sunday spaghetti supper, I prayed real fast he'd say yes.

"That's really nice of you, Ms. Turner, but—"

We were near the door, right in front of a row of phone booths. "Why don't you call home and ask if it's okay?" my ma said, fishing in her handbag for dimes.

"Oh, that's all right." He quickly took some out of his pocket. "I don't really have to call, I know it'll be okay, but—" He shrugged and started for the booth, then turned back to us. "Are you sure it's no trouble?"

"Absolutely positive," my ma said. "As long as you like spaghetti."

"*Do* I! It's my favorite!"

"Me too!" I cried. "And wait till you taste her sauce. It's her specialty."

He snapped his fingers. "Well, then, that does it!"

Raymond was a funny guy. He would talk a blue streak, about all kinds of stuff—mostly things he had read—but then he'd suddenly turn around and start asking us nonstop questions. Especially when he found out we were from New York. "Oh, man, I can't wait to go there!" he told us on his third helping of spaghetti. My ma's sauce was really great, and Raymond had lots of places to put food. "It must have everything Chicago doesn't have."

"It sure does," my ma said. "Garbage and graffiti."

He hooted with laughter. "Well, our weather makes up for that. Anyway, one of these days I'm going to head east, just to see. Which do you like better, Danny, here or there?"

He always asked questions like that; half the time I didn't even know how to answer, but I liked being asked. He was interested in what I thought about things. In a lot of ways he treated me like someone his own age. I liked that, too. And other times, he treated me like a kid brother. And I liked that. A lot.

When we finished eating he jumped up to help clear the table, just the way he helped serve the food; and when my ma started washing the dishes, he snapped up the towel and said, "Got another one for yourself, Danny?" So the three of us stood there in the kitchen doing the dishes as if it was something we'd done together all our lives.

"Tell me about your family, Raymond," my ma said as she dipped into the suds.

"I have this whole bunch of little brothers and sisters," he began, explaining that his mother had died when he was nine and his father remarried the next year. "All of a sudden, after being an only child, I started having a great big family." He shook his head. "Weird."

"That must have been nice for you," my ma said.

He shrugged. "Yeah, sometimes. But it's always so noisy and hectic." The youngest were two-year-old twins, and the others were four and six. "Most of the time the apartment is like a little circus. Sounds, smells, close quarters—but not that much fun. If the kids aren't crying, the TV is blaring. Or both. Ychh!" And he shuddered. "To tell you the truth, half the time I feel as though I'm just taking up a lot of extra space that they don't have enough of to begin with. So"—and he laughed—"I figure the best thing I can do for all of them is stay out of their way as much as I can."

"Oh, Raymond," my ma said, "how can you say that! I'm sure it must be nice to have someone like you around." I knew she liked his good manners and how helpful he was.

He snorted. "No, I don't think they exactly see it that way. I eat too much and always have my nose in a book and never help enough with the kids . . . so I just make it easier for all of us by finding, uh, more congenial places to grace my presence with."

"Like," my ma said, grinning, "museums."

"Like," he repeated with the same grin, *"the* museum." He took a deep, sort of shaky breath.

"Man, I grew up in that place! It's what got me interested in scientific stuff. My mom started taking me there when I was little. By the time I was Danny's age I knew the place like the back of my hand. Then," and he shrugged, "when things got more and more crowded around the house, I started going back."

My ma was scrubbing away at the saucepot, and I kept drying the last plate over and over. Finally my ma said, "Well, I'm sure glad you were there today, Raymond."

Suddenly the kitchen light started flickering, and we all laughed, as if it was a signal to end being so serious. "Hey," Raymond said, squinting up at it, "I'll see if I can fix that. Do you have a stepstool?"

"That's okay, you can just stand on the chair," my ma told him. "It started doing that yesterday but it's getting worse. We probably need a new bulb." It was one of those round fluorescent lights.

Raymond was up on the chair now, checking the bulb. "H'mm, just as I thought—it's the starter. Nothing much—I'll pick one up at the hardware store tomorrow if you want."

"Oh, thank you, Raymond, but I'm sure the super will take care of it," my ma said. "But listen, you're welcome to come and visit whenever you like, Raymond."

"Yeah," I chimed in. He lived about a half-mile away, and his school was only a few blocks from mine. "Maybe we can meet after school sometime."

He pushed at my shoulder and gave his croaky laugh. "Hey, yeah, good idea. How about tomorrow?"

"You have yourself a new friend," my ma said after he left, smiling. "I can't help it. I know we haven't known him very long, but there's something about him—he's like one of the family."

"Yeah," I said. We were both quiet for a couple minutes. I took a deep breath, then burst out laughing.

"What?" she said, her eyes sparkling; she knew I was going to come up with something special.

"Did it ever hit you what Raymond did to us?"

Her smile vanished. *"Did* to us? What do you mean?"

"He picked us up at the museum. He started telling us all those interesting facts. He got himself invited to lunch. He reminded me of someone right away, but at first I couldn't put my finger on it. Then he got himself invited home to supper—"

"But we *liked* him. We *wanted* him."

"I know, I know!" I was still laughing; she was still looking confused.

"You make it sound so—so *figured-out."*

"Who should know better than me? Ma, he worked his MO on us!"

"His—*oh-h-h!"* And now she started giggling.

"I figured it out by the time that egg hatched who it was he reminded me of."

"You!" she cried.

I grinned at her. "Maybe that's why I like him so much."

She hugged me. "Me too. I guess kindred souls gravitate together."

"Huh? What does *that* mean? Boy, you're getting to talk like him!"

She giggled. "Oh, you know—people who are alike just naturally drift toward each other."

I thought about that and decided it was probably true. In some ways. "He sure liked being with us, didn't he? Do you think it's because it's so awful at his house?"

She smiled. "I'd rather think it's because he enjoys our company more. And maybe a little bit because you remind him of himself at your age."

I shrugged. "Like I said before, he worked a pretty good MO—just like me."

"Maybe that's why I like him so much—you're two of a kind. Anyhow"—and she grabbed me and hugged me—"what an easy way to have a made-to-order big brother!"

Chapter 3

Did you ever notice how things that happen in your life often come together in a funny way? The kind of stuff that people call a coincidence. My ma calls it Fate, and I believe it. I mean, you couldn't win an argument over it with a scientist or anything —but you must feel it in your bones that something is going on somewhere to make all this stuff just keep *happening*. Well, that's the way it was from that very next day on. It all started in social studies, first period after lunch.

Now, you wouldn't think anything as dull-sounding as learning about the Renaissance period of history could set up a whole chain of flukes, would you? But there I was, still tasting the last drops of chocolate milk at the corners of my mouth from the school cafeteria and wondering if Mr. Greeley ever played checkers on the tie he was wearing that day when he said something that really caught my interest. He had just started telling our class about the Renaissance in Europe and explained how to pronounce it, and all, and everyone was looking pretty bored, getting set for the deep freeze.

Frank, the guy across from me, gave one of

those long, loud yawns, and of course everyone laughed; but Mr. Greeley didn't get mad, the way a lot of teachers do. He just stood there and looked around at everyone, real slow and careful, and the room got quieter and quieter. He has these piercing dark eyes, and he fastened them on Frank as he said, going from a whisper to a shout: "You can't imagine what an exciting time it was in the world!"

Then he went on real softly, so we all had to strain to hear: "It was like plodding through a jungle of dark ignorance and suddenly coming out into a clearing of brilliant light, where there was music and art and the beginnings of scientific investigation." Now he roared: "*Renaissance*—a rebirth! The world was being born again, on a higher level than it had been for hundreds of years!"

It was pretty exciting to see the way he was reacting to this whole idea. Maybe because he got so worked up about it, it was like the feeling you get at ball games when you know a big play is coming up. You could just see that everyone was tensing up for Mr. Greeley's big delivery. Suddenly those dark piercing eyes were focusing on me. "Danny! Did you ever hear the expression 'He's a Renaissance Man'?"

I shrugged and shook my head. "No."

Everyone laughed.

He looked around the room. "Did anyone else?"

Smartypants Hugh Folwell raised his hand. "I think I did."

"Do you know what it means?"

"No."

Everyone laughed again. Now Mr. Greeley grinned. "Well, I'm relieved. If you had, you would have ruined my whole show."

He had us all by then. We were practically on the edge of our seats while he explained what it was like in those times when there was such a big breakthrough in learning and so many new ideas. That's when he told us how the expression Renaissance Man came about. It's what they call a person who has talents in a lot of different fields—one of those guys everyone always wants to be like. They know about science and books and sports, music and art and medicine—you name it.

"I thought that's called a genius," Kathy said, and a lot of kids were nodding, showing that's what they had thought, too.

Mr. Greeley tugged at his tie, the way he does when he gets excited. "It's different. Geniuses are people who have very high IQ's—every genius *could* be a Renaissance Man if he wanted to, but not every Renaissance Man is a genius. It depends on how you use your intelligence."

"Mr. Greeley," Susan piped up, "can't a Renaissance Man be a woman?"

There was a big burst of laughter—mostly from the guys—and a whole lot of buzzing and *"All right!"* yells from the girls.

Mr. Greeley stood leaning against his desk, his arms folded, a big grin making his eyes sparkle. "I was wondering how long it would take for that!"

He nodded at her approvingly now. "You're absolutely right, Susan. And in modern times, no question about it—it's just another example of our sexist ways of thinking. But the fact is that between the fourteenth and sixteenth centuries, women didn't have the opportunity to become Renaissance—ah, er—persons."

Everyone was cracking up now, and then there was a whole big discussion about what sexist means, and before long the battle lines were just about drawn between the guys and girls in class.

All the while Mr. Greeley just stood there watching and listening; but the moment it got to be a free-for-all, he put up his hand and said real loud: "Enough! Now that your brains are working, let's learn about this fascinating period in the history of our world. Shh, calm down, we'll explore it together. And—" and he looked around with that searching stare of his—"if you pay attention to this whole concept, one day you, too, will be Renaissance Men and Women." There was a burst of applause, and he gave one of those short nods that means, "Okay, now that we understand each other, let's get on with the job." And from that moment on, Mr. Greeley was my favorite teacher.

Now, the flukey thing that happened was with Raymond. He was waiting for me outside after school, the way we had planned the day before at my house; and almost before I could open my mouth he said, "Hey, Danny, how would you like to go to a wrestling meet?"

"Now?"

"Yes, over at the high school."

"Sure, that sounds like fun. I didn't know you liked wrestling."

"One of my friends is on the team."

"Oh," says I, "so that's why."

"Well, it's only one of the reasons. But I really like the sport. I *respect* it. If I had more discipline, I'd go out for it."

"You mean about practicing and stuff?" I tried to keep step with his giant strides, but it wasn't easy. It made me feel proud, walking along with a teenager like that.

"Well, that, too, but that's the easier part," he was saying. "No, I mean the really, really tough self-discipline of keeping yourself in physical and mental and spiritual shape. It's a very demanding sport, you know."

I shrugged. "Well, I don't know too much about it, except for the horsing around I've done with my friends. I was pretty good at a full nelson when I was in Cub Scouts, but we were just little twerps then."

"Yeah?" He was sizing me up, I could tell. "H'mm, you might make a pretty good wrestler. You certainly have the build for it—wiry and spare. If you stay that way."

"Do you think so?"

He laughed. "Well, there are a lot of other important factors, too: coordination, agility, timing. It's really a—a symphony of action—" He stopped suddenly.

"What's wrong?"

"The look on your face. Sorry, Danny, I get carried away sometimes—you'll learn that about me."

"But I like it!" I burst out. "I like it when you talk like an encyclopedia!"

He gave my shoulder a rough shove. "Huh, that shows how much *you* know. If you don't recognize a Renaissance Man when you bump up against one, you've got a lot to learn, fella."

I stopped dead, right in the middle of the street, and screeched: *"I don't believe it, I don't believe it!"*

He looked around, startled. "What? What's wrong?" Then, as a car approached, he grabbed my arm and yanked me over to the sidewalk.

"What did you say before, Raymond? If I don't recognize a *what?*"

He thought for a moment, then said, "Renaissance Man. I bet you never heard of that, did you?"

I gave him a play punch in the belly. "Oh, you do, hey? Well, Mr. Professor, it just so happens I *have* heard of it. In fact, I can give you a whole big definition of it and all about the Renaissance period that came right after the Middle Ages, and—"

"Whoa, okay, okay! You're a pretty smart little feller, I could see that right away. Hey, I never asked you, Danny: what do you want to be when you grow up?"

We were standing in front of the door to the high school gym. I scratched my head and looked at him seriously. "I never really knew till this afternoon. But I want to be like you. A Renaissance Man."

"Yo, Raymond, how's it going?"

I thought it was a girl at first, because of all the frizzy blond curls. He even had baby-blue eyes.

"Bones!" Raymond cried, and they shook each other happily. "Hey, I want you to meet my good friend, Danny." He turned to me. "This is Millard Marrow, but we call him 'Bones'."

He stuck out his hand and took mine in a grip of iron. "Real glad to know you, Danny. Going to watch us?"

He was carrying a gym bag. "Are you a wrestler?" I asked. He was a lot shorter than Raymond and skinny.

He laughed, holding the door open for me. "Yeah, don't I look it?"

"Bones!" someone yelled as we walked in, saving me from answering. "Hurry up!" He ran off with a smile and a wave, and Raymond chuckled. "That Bones, he's really something. We've gone to school together since kindergarten."

"Where did he get that funny name?" I asked Raymond. "Is it because he's skinny and his bones stick out?"

He snapped his fingers in the air. "You *are* a smart kid—I never noticed that! But actually, it's his name—Marrow. You know, marrow bones. The kind you use for soup. Some wiseacre kid in third grade started it—the funny thing is, he was on the fat side then—and anyway it just stuck. Besides, he always liked it, because—well, just think if your name was Millard."

I laughed. "I guess he could thank that kid." I had never heard of marrow bones before, but I always say, live and learn.

"Anyway," Raymond said, "wait till you see him in action. He's a powerhouse."

We were in the gym, and when I looked around at the kids from both schools who had come to support their team, I saw I was about the only one my age there. Raymond knew a lot of the guys from his school and some of them came over to say hello. He always introduced me, and they all asked if I was his brother. The first time, he gave me a little wink as he answered, "Not exactly." After that he said the same thing, but he didn't wink. Boy, did that make me feel good!

The first two matches were pretty good, especially for me, because I'd never seen any before. Raymond kept explaining about the different holds and the scoring all through the first two matches, so by the third one, when Bones came out, I understood pretty much. I got really excited watching him, and I could see that Raymond did, too. Bones and his opponent were very evenly matched—they practically could have doubled for each other in build—and at the beginning they did just about the same things and kept scoring even. Then Bones started winning all the points. His power just seemed to build by the moment, and the other guy dwindled. And then, in a flash, Bones had him pinned. Raymond and I both jumped up and yelled a cheer before we even realized what we were doing.

"You did well, Bones, you did well," Raymond told him later, shaking his hand real hard while he clapped him on the shoulder. Their team won by four points, and the locker room was noisy and crowded by the time we got there after the match. Bones asked us to wait till he showered and changed. He came out looking like—well, with his blond curls all fluffed up from the shower and his baby-blue eyes shining with victory, he sure didn't look like a prize wrestler!

"Well, my little friend," Bones said to me now, "how did you like it?"

"It was great! You were really terrific, Bones. Congratulations!"

"Thanks, Danny." Suddenly he started sizing me up. "Hey, you interested in doing some wrestling? Bet you'd be good at it. Want me to show you some holds?" Before I could answer, he turned to Raymond. "What do you say we go for some pizza?"

"You?" Raymond said. "Go for *pizza?* I thought you couldn't go off your diet of string beans and raisins, or whatever it is that keeps you in condition."

Bones laughed. "I'll go off it for you guys—it's a special occasion. Want to?"

Raymond shrugged. "Sure. How about you, Danny? Want to come?"

I stuck my hand in my pocket and turned a thin, hard dime in my fingers. "Gee, I'd like to, but—"

Bones grinned down at me. "We'll treat—right, Raymond?"

"Sure. Come on, Danny—we'll call your mother and tell her we'll bring you home afterwards." He turned to Bones. "Danny just moved out here from New York so he doesn't know his way around so well yet."

"That's real nice of you guys—"

"You're from New York?" Bones was saying, staring at me funny. "Oh, man, do I have to talk to you! Hey, wait till you taste our Chicago pizza!"

I called my ma at work right from the school gym, and Raymond got on the phone with her when she started making noises about school nights and homework and stuff, and he gave her a whole long promise of looking out for me and bringing me home early and all—that, after all, he had to do his homework, too. That clinched it.

We met Chicky Fontina on our way to the pizza place. He was a friend of Bones's, and he said sure when they invited him along. They all thought I was pretty funny, a lot of it because of my New York accent, I guess; but I didn't care because I felt like about the most important twelve-year-old kid in the world being with these guys—a wrestling champ, a Renaissance Man, and a future rock music star.

I couldn't believe my luck, stumbling into this whole circle of high school guys who let me tag along with them; and as I listened to Chicky talk about the rock group he was in and how it made all those years of music lessons worthwhile, I suddenly remembered about that Renaissance Man thing and how just the day before I'd never even heard the term and now with all these new friends I was on my way to becoming one. Maybe even to getting to be as smart as Raymond someday.

"Do you play anything, Danny?" Chicky asked me after we ordered our pizza. Chicky was small with dark hair and dark eyes that seemed to dart around looking at everything all the time. He chewed gum and drummed his fingers on the table—everything about him looked like it was moving.

"You mean music? No—I tried drums when I was a little kid, but the neighbors threatened to have us evicted so I switched to baseball."

"Well, you're still plenty young enough to start again. Why don't you try another instrument?"

"Like what?" I saw myself playing in a rock band and the audience screaming, "Danny, we love you!" But I couldn't picture what I was playing.

Chicky shrugged. "Guitar—what else?" The others laughed, and I realized that was his instrument. "Listen, you guys," he went on, "we're doing a concert Friday night at a school on the North Side. How about coming?"

"Can you get us in free?" Bones asked.

Chicky thought for a moment. "I think I can swing it. You could be our prop men."

"Does that mean we'll have to work?"

"Well, you can help set up if you want to."

"Sure I'd want to," Raymond said. "I'm good at it, too. I like fooling around with the wiring."

"Me too," I piped up.

They all looked at me in surprise. "You know how?"

I shrugged. "No, but I learn fast."

They liked that. They liked the yucky pizza, too; and when they asked me if I'd ever had any like it before, I said, "No. I never even knew you could make pizza this way. It's so different from any I ever had." It had a tremendously thick crust and enough cheese to paralyze your tongue.

"Oh, that's our special Chicago deep-dish pizza," Bones told me proudly. "It's famous!"

"No wonder," I cracked, "anything as strange as this would *have* to be famous." They hooted at that as I added quickly, not wanting to insult my new friends who, after all, were treating me, too: "It's good, though. Real interesting stuff."

Chicky shook his head, smiling. "That's the first time I ever heard anyone call pizza interesting. Listen, how would you like to learn guitar? I could show you a few things sometime." Before I could even answer, he turned to Raymond. "Hey, man, it's nice to see you come out of your shell. I didn't know you and Bones were buddies."

I could see a light pink color rising in Raymond's face, but Bones, laughing, just said, "We weren't, not since grade school. But we ran into each other today, and he and Danny were my private little fan club. Hey"—and he clapped Raymond on the shoulder—"remember in fourth grade when we tried to build a rocket?"

They both started laughing while they told us about how the styrofoam kept shredding, and Chicky just shook his head. "A couple of crazy guys," he said, winking at me. "So, what are you, anyhow—the mascot?"

"Well, in a way. But more of a good-luck charm."

Bones made a circle with his thumb and forefinger. "Right on! That's why I won my match."

I was double-happy: for myself, being taken into their group like that; and for Raymond, because I realized the same thing was happening to him, too. These weren't special friends of his after all, just guys he knew. Like all those other people he knew who came over to say hello at the wrestling meet. You could tell everyone liked him, but now I realized none was a special friend. When Chicky said that about coming out of his shell, I got the feeling Raymond was a guy who pretty much stuck by himself. Till now. But the way Bones and Chicky were opening up to him, I could see that was changing.

As I was telling my ma about all the things that had happened to me that day, a lot of it sounded almost like out of a dream, starting with Mr. Greeley and his Renaissance lecture. And then Raymond calling himself a Renaissance Man, sort of as a joke, but in a way that made me realize it was true for him.

"The weird thing is," I told her, "if Raymond had said that to me just one day sooner, I wouldn't have known what he was talking about. I never even heard the word before in my whole life!"

"I've had things like that happen to me, too. Isn't it spooky?"

When I saw that she didn't laugh at me and was really interested, I told her how I decided it was what I wanted to be, too: smart, like Raymond, and knowing how to do a lot of different kinds of things. And how I'd never have had any idea of how to go about it, but there it all was, one, two, three, falling right into my lap just because I met Raymond.

As I talked about it, I realized how smart he was just knowing how to learn whatever he wanted to. But he was sixteen, and I was only twelve. I wondered if I could ever catch up to him; and then I realized that through him, and through his friends, I was taking a shortcut: in one day, I'd met two new people and, even without asking, had them offering to teach me two new things. At that rate, I figured, I might be able to make it by sixteen. But I had to lay the groundwork.

First I told her about all my adventures—oh, I didn't leave out anything. "There was so much of that thick, sticky cheese in that crazy pizza it stuck to the roof of my mouth and my tongue, and I got scared my mouth would lock shut!"

By now she was laughing so much she was almost crying. I told her, then, about Raymond starting to get to be buddies with these guys, and she shook her head in wonder. "Isn't it funny how one little chance meeting will set off a whole chain of events? Wow, Danny, you really are his good luck charm!" She smiled. "And he's yours!"

"Anyway, Ma," I went on, "I hope you understand that this is the opportunity of a lifetime for me. I want to be somebody special—somebody great. But you're going to have to let me do all these things with these guys." I explained about Bones offering to teach me wrestling and Chicky to teach me guitar. "After all, I'm not a little kid anymore. But you'll have to trust me."

She put her hand on my shoulder and smiled at me, her eyes big and serious. "I do, Danny. And I know how important this is to you. Don't worry, honey, we'll work it all out, as long as you're always honest with me. And you have to trust me and my judgment, too."

"I do, Ma, I do."

"Well, then, there shouldn't be any problems. Sometimes I'll just come along so I can keep up with what you're doing."

"We-ell—"

"Trust goes only so far, Danny."

"But *Ma*—they're sixteen. They'll think I'm a baby if I bring my mother along!"

She shrugged. "Suppose your mother wants to learn, too? Suppose she wants to become a Renaissance Woman?"

"Oh, *Ma* . . ."

She laughed. "Don't worry, I'm not interested in

the wrestling. But the rock concert—that's something I could relate to."

I looked at her and shrugged. Why bother arguing about it now—maybe she'd forget about it by Friday.

Chapter 4

With the way the rest of the week went, I almost forgot about it myself by Friday. The next couple days Raymond was outside waiting for me after school, and we went over to watch wrestling practice. Wednesday he and Bones walked me home, and Bones started teaching me some wrestling moves and holds.

"You're a natural," he told me after the second session.

"Thanks, Bones. You're a good teacher. Listen, I really appreciate that you're taking the time and all."

He bent over and put his hands on my shoulders. "Hey, Danny, I'll tell you a secret: I always wondered what it would be like having a kid brother to teach and coach."

Raymond walked in on that. "Well, what's it like, Bones?"

He straightened up, laughing. "Much better than being one!"

They were still there when my ma got home from work, and she asked if they wanted to stay to supper. "That is, if you like brown rice and tofu and spinach salad," she said, with a sort of sheepish smile.

"That's fantastic!" Bones cried. "I just started learning about that stuff—our coach is a health food nut and keeps trying to push it. Then my sister became a veggie and started making all that glop for me and her, and my mom's always fighting with her about it."

"What's a veggie?" I asked.

"What I've decided to become since our trip to the museum," my ma said. "A vegetarian."

"A veg—hey, you're kidding!" I cried.

"Haven't you noticed?" she said slyly. "No more hamburgers and hot dogs around here."

"But you only said you were cutting out junk food. We had—" I scratched my head, and a parade of the week's meals marched by: tuna casserole, spinach-cheese-and-onion pie. And salad. Salad with bean sprouts and all kinds of vegetables that I'd never even seen before, till I complained I was going to turn into a rabbit, and my ma just laughed and told me how good they were for me and how much roughage and Vitamin E and C and all kinds of other crazy things they had. *Remember what that exhibit said at the museum?* blah-blah-blah, till I threw up my hands and said, "Okay, okay, next time let's go to the McDonald's Museum," and she said, "I've never heard of that one, is it in Chicago?" and I said, "Yes, and it has these terrific exhibits of all kinds of hamburgers with every healthy vegetable and salad on it, and ketchup and mustard, too. And you'd be surprised, it's cheaper than eating at home." She just laughed at that and ruffled my hair and said mysteriously, "Don't worry, honey, you'll get used to it."

I was too busy to take it seriously at the time. But now, here she was trading gasps with Bones over all this weirdo food stuff and then telling me she's become a vegetarian, so I can only wonder out loud: "Where does that leave me if you're a veggie?" I pick up language fast.

She giggled. "Right with me, Danny—and on the way to becoming the healthiest kid in the Midwest. How about it, fellows—want to help me put the supper together? Use the phone to call your folks."

Bones made it fast, pushing up his sleeves as he came back. "Okay, let's get started." As he and my ma headed for the kitchen, I heard Raymond saying into the phone, "What's for supper tonight? Oh. Well, I think I'll stay over at my friend Danny's. I've been invited. They're having something that sounds better, and Bones is staying, too, so I'll see you later."

I didn't have the nerve to ask him what they were having at home, but I sure was curious, especially when I saw his face as he tasted the tofu. I said it for both of us: "Yuck! What *is* this, anyway?"

"The most protein with the lowest carbohydrates," my ma recited proudly. So *that* was why she brought that strange cookbook home!

"Well, you can have your tofu," I said, "but I'm

going to have me some eggs. What about you, Raymond? Want a mess of scrambled?"

I could see he was embarrassed. "That sounds pretty good. What me to make 'em?"

We both looked at my ma, and I could just tell Raymond was remembering the same thing I was: my ma at the museum after she saw the chick hatched and promised she'd never eat eggs again. But she just smiled and said, "Smart boy, Raymond. If you ever tasted Danny's scrambled eggs, you'd never want to eat them again either."

Bones cracked up, and I just smiled. "I only need a little practice, Ma—don't worry, I'll improve. Wait till you see what good hamburgers I can make!"

"I've got a special technique for scrambled eggs," Raymond put in tactfully. "Come on, Danny, I'll show you."

He really did. What he did, he practically burned the butter before he threw the beat-up eggs in the skillet—lots of butter. The eggs came out golden brown and soft and delicious. Then they both made Ma go in and watch TV while we cleaned up. After they left she said, "They're darlings! You're lucky, Danny—you've got yourself a couple of big brothers made to order. At the rate you're going, we'll end up with a huge family!"

The next day Raymond wasn't waiting for me after school, or anyone else, either. He and Bones had been talking about checking out some equipment with Chicky as they were leaving my house, but after all their thanking they didn't say anything to me except, "See you, Danny." Now as I walked home, I started going over my new plan in my head, the one about being a Renaissance Man. I thought about how I had made such a good start, but it hit me then that I couldn't depend on just one source to get me everywhere I wanted to go. Raymond was pretty smart, and he had a lot of contacts, but I had to do something on my own, too. After all, I'd run a pretty clever operation back in New York with my whole string of zoodaddies, and they were grown men, so I certainly could work up something with a bunch of teenagers. Like that one over in the driveway, standing there staring at an old van with its hood open. It was a faded blue with pictures painted on its sides—a sunset and a cactus on one side, and a mountain and a lake on the other. As I got up close, I could see this kid—he was about Raymond's age—shaking his head and pursing his lips the way people do when they can't figure out something.

I stopped. "What's wrong with it?"

He did that with his mouth once more and then scratched his head. "Darned if I know. I could have sworn it was the battery, but I charged it up, and it still won't start." He was wearing a quilted vest over a thermal undershirt, and there were grease stains on his sleeves and jeans. He pushed his heavy glasses back up with his long, slender, dark fingers and bent over to examine the battery. He had to bend a lot because he was about twice as tall as I.

I stuck my head in next to his: "Hey, look at the way that wire is pulled away." I pointed at the right side where it was separated from the lug.

The kid bent closer, then yelled, "Hey, that's it! That battery cable is sure enough busted!" He turned around to look at me carefully. "You're a pretty smart kid. How old are you, anyway?"

"Twelve." I tried not to smile too big.

He held out his hand for a "give-me-five." "You're okay, buddy. Want to take a trip with me to the auto parts store?"

Well, I had me a new friend, Tom St. George.

"It's my brother's van," he explained, swinging along beside me with his long, loping gait, "but I'm the only one in the family who knows how to fix it, so I get to use it a lot." He clapped my shoulder. "Soon as I get it going I'll take you for a ride. After all," and he laughed, "without you, I'd never have found out what was wrong with it."

That's the way Tom was. I mean, in another minute he would have noticed it himself, but he gave me all the credit. Even to the man who sold him the new cable. "My little buddy here found out the cable was busted, how do you like that?" he said as the man put it in a bag.

The man smiled. "Seems to me any moron could have figured it out."

"Oh yeah?" I said. "It wasn't really busted—you could almost hardly tell . . ."

Now the man laughed. "Okay, kid, okay." He said to Tom, nodding his head at me, "This your expert? I wish you luck, fella."

Tom peered at him, saying seriously, "Thanks,

we really appreciate your help. Come on, Danny."

"Why was he so mean?" I asked outside.

Tom shrugged. "I don't know. Maybe because he thought we were being fresh. Or maybe because I'm black. Or maybe just because he's mean."

"Or maybe all three."

"Hey, you're a pretty smart kid. Are you really only twelve?"

When I asked him how he learned to fix cars, he said he had always loved to tinker and just seemed to be able to figure out how to fix things. But his special love had always been cars and he started hanging around mechanics at garages from the time he was my age. "Soon as I get enough money to start buying the parts, I'm going to build my own car."

"Honest? Wow! You mean from scratch?"

He smiled. "I guess you could say that. I'm going to buy a chassis and get used parts and put it together." He figured he had about half the money saved from the handyman and repair jobs he did for people in the neighborhood, his teachers, and his family's friends. He was the youngest of a big family, and when he found out about me, he shook his head and smiled. "Man, it must be nice and quiet in your house."

"Come over and see. It's only a few blocks down from yours."

By the time we got back to his house, we felt like old friends. I helped him open the van hood and watched, fascinated, as he replaced the broken cable. He worked like such a pro!

"I wish I could do things like that. It doesn't even *look* easy!"

He laughed. "Oh, come on, Danny, it's not hard! I bet it wouldn't be for you, not the way you handle yourself. Listen"—and he shoved at me playfully—"if you play your cards right, maybe I'll let you work on my car with me."

"Honest?" I thought my eyes would pop out of my head.

He slammed the hood closed and hopped up into the van, yelling, "Say your best prayer, Danny!" and he switched on the ignition key, floored the accelerator, and *phwoom!* It started!

"Eeyow!" he yelled, then turned to me with a big grin. "How about a ride home, buddy? You're my regular little old mascot!"

As we're pulling up in front of my building, who comes walking down the street from the bus stop but my ma.

"Your mother?" Tom repeated, staring at her as she came closer and started looking shocked when she saw me hop out of this funky van. "Wow!"

I felt pretty proud of both of them. "Ma, this is my new friend, Tom St. George. I helped him fix his van."

She invited him in, but he said no, he had to get home for supper. Then he turned to me. "Hey, Danny, there's a big auto show this weekend at the Navy Pier. Want to go on Saturday?"

I looked at my ma and she smiled. "It's okay

with me. Let me know how much the tickets are."

"Oh, that's okay, Mrs. Turner. A friend of mine gave me passes. How about twelve o'clock, Danny? We'll want to get there early, there's lots to see."

"How do you *do* it?" she said as she unlocked our door. "Every time I turn around, you have a new friend. But why are they all so old? What's wrong with kids your age?"

I shrugged. "Nothing. But they're just not as interesting."

She narrowed her eyes. "Are you still hooked on that Renaissance Man stuff?" She hugged me. "Oh, Danny, you're too much!"

"Hey, Ma, who's Wayne?" I was looking at the name under Friday on the appointment calendar hanging near our kitchen door.

"Remember that policeman who brought you home the day you were lost?"

"The Mustache?"

She laughed. "Is that what you called him? Well, you're not going to believe this, but he was in the store where I was doing a demonstration yesterday—off duty. I didn't even recognize him, out of uniform and all. Anyway, we got to talking, and he asked me out for Friday."

I shook my head. "Well, how about that!" I shrugged. "Okay, he seems like a pretty nice guy." I smiled, then said, "Too bad you won't be able to go to that rock concert with me and the guys." I had my fingers crossed behind my back.

She gasped. "I forgot all about it! Oh, well, I know Raymond and Bones well enough by now, so I'm sure you'll be okay. Whatever happened to Chicky and those music lessons he was going to give you?"

"He was real busy this week practicing for the concert."

"I guess so. What's the group's name, anyway?"

"Four Brothers and a Sister."

"Oooh, I like that! Who's the sister?"

"Chicky's sister Dimples. She's fifteen and just starting out. They say she's terrific."

"Well, it's really nice that they have such good family feeling. I'm going to make their next concert, I promise. I can't wait to hear them." She thought for a moment. *"Dimples!* What a lucky kid she is! At her age I would have given my right arm to sing with a group!"

"Honest? I never knew it was that important to you!" I thought of how she was always singing along with albums and the radio and stuff, and how she was trying to be an actress, but I never knew she wanted to be a singer, too.

"I'd still like a crack at it. Maybe the Four Brothers and a Sister will let me do a number with them sometime."

I laughed. I could just see that.

"Why does everyone you know have a nick-name?" she was asking now. "Don't they like their real names?"

"I don't even know what Chicky's real name is. But if your name was Millard, wouldn't you use a nickname?"

She laughed. "Maybe. But it wouldn't be Bones."

"Raymond doesn't have one either."

"No, Raymond wouldn't, would he? Not even Ray."

"I know what you mean. He *is* sort of the formal type."

"It's kind of nice. I think he's a very good influence on you, Danny."

I didn't say anything else, because I didn't want to spoil it. I was just so glad she wasn't going to be able to come to check up on me I didn't even say how I felt about people being a good influence on me.

So everything was cool. I was going to a rock concert with my friends, and my ma was going out on a date with The Mustache. Raymond phoned that night to tell me everyone was meeting at Chicky's house at six-thirty on Friday to get all the group's stuff together to take over to the concert. "Can you be ready at six? I'll come by for you," he said, explaining Chicky's older brother was going to drive all of us in his station wagon.

I didn't expect to see him waiting outside for me after school on Friday. "Hi, Raymond." He looked real worried. "Something wrong?"

"Chicky's brother's station wagon broke down,

so they don't have any way of getting the equipment over there."

"What are they going to do?"

"Well, everyone's working on it. Two of the guys' fathers have small cars, so they're going to try to get the stuff into them and maybe they'll have to make two trips. I have to go along because I'm going to set up for them, but I don't think there'll be room for you, Danny."

I shrugged. Life was full of disappointments, someone said once. Full of bright ideas, too. "Hey, I know someone with a van. Want me to ask him if he'll help out?"

Raymond's face lit up like a pinball machine. "*Do* I! Oh, man, that would be great, Danny. You'd be a real hero!"

We went straight over to Tom's house, and guess who was stretched out in the driveway, underneath the van. I tugged at the toe of his sneaker. "Hey, Tom, what're you doing?"

A muffled voice floated up to us. "Playing backgammon—want to join me?"

"Hey, no kidding, can you come out for a minute? It's important." I was bending down yelling to him.

He wriggled out from under, his thermal undershirt and quilted vest and face and hands all the same color now—grease. As soon as he saw it was me, he lit into a big grin. "Hiya, Danny, what's up?" He stood up and reached into the van for a rag and started wiping off his hands, then his glasses, then his face, as I introduced him to Raymond. He stuck out his hand, then looked at it apologetically. "Real glad to know you, Raymond, but, uh, I wouldn't touch me if I was you."

Raymond shrugged, smiled, and grabbed it in a thumbs-up handshake. "Any friend of Danny's is a friend of mine."

Tom clapped him on the shoulder. "Well, hey, ditto, man!"

I just smiled. But boy, did I feel good!

"What's wrong with the van?" Raymond asked.

"Nothing. I was just checking out the muffler. One of the clamps was a little loose was all. Hey, you guys want to go for a test ride?"

"We-ell," Raymond said, "not right now, but—" He looked at me.

"Listen, Tom," I said, "how would you like to go to a rock concert tonight, free?"

"What's the deal?"

"Well," I went on, "it's like this. We're in a real jam. . . ."

He said yes, if it was okay with his brother, and went in the house to call him at work when we explained we had to know pretty soon.

Raymond shook his head like crazy when Tom came back out with a victory signal. "You're a lucky charm, Danny!"

Tom laughed. "That's what I told him—right?" He grinned at me.

My ma's daily note was on the hall table:

"Wayne is coming at 7 and taking me out to dinner. Heat up the leftover eggplant casserole and make yourself a nice salad. Take your vitamins and dust the living room. I'll be home before you leave. Love, Ma."

I did everything she said except make a salad. I figured the vitamins would take care of that. Then I took a shower and put on a sort of fancy shirt and my good jeans and clean sneakers. I still had some time till Raymond would be there, so I flopped on the couch with my ten-year-old copy of the *World Almanac* I picked up for a quarter. It seemed like a good way to start rounding out my education, and a lot faster than reading the encyclopedia, the way Raymond liked to do. And it was even better being so old because I could learn about history that was written right when it happened instead of all that boring stuff made up a long time later. The book had all kinds of facts and tables and things that didn't mean very much, but there was a lot of real good stuff, like an article about what it was going to be like in the next hundred years, with underground cities and vacation trips to the moon for no-gravity fun. As I lay there dreaming about transferring space capsules when I wanted to travel from one planet to another —sort of like getting a transfer from the crosstown bus when I lived in New York—the phone rang, and Raymond's voice brought me back down to earth in a hurry.

"Danny, we have another crisis. Do you have Tom's phone number? It's not in the book."

"No. What's wrong, another transportation problem?" I was all ready to joke about getting a rocket.

"Something even worse. Chicky's sister is sick and can't sing tonight."

"Dimples? What's wrong with her?"

He gave an unfunny laugh. "Would you believe chicken pox?"

"I had that when I was a little kid. Hey, I bet if she wore a high neck and long sleeves and lots of makeup no one would know . . ."

"Oh, Danny, you're as bad as I am. When I said that to Chicky, he told me she has a real sore throat and fever, so there's no way. Anyhow, all the guys are scouting around frantically trying to dig up someone to take her place, and I'm supposed to tell Tom we need more time. I know he has a phone because he went in and called his brother, remember? It must be unlisted."

"Well, it's no problem," I said, real cool. "I'll just run over to his house and tell him. It's only a couple blocks up. What time is it, anyway?"

"Five-thirty. Tell him to hang on, and we'll let him know what's happening. And oh, Danny—"

"I know, get his phone number."

"Yep, that's right. Smart kid. And ask him if he knows anyone who can sing. Maybe he has a sister or something."

"Okay."

"Take my phone number and call me as soon as you get back, okay?"

My ma walked in just as I was putting on my coat, and of course she started with the questions and I had to tell her the whole story.

"Listen, I have to hurry and get over to Tom's as fast as I can, they need his phone number, and I have to see if he knows anyone who can sing. Maybe one of his sisters, or . . ." My ma had this funny look on her face, and I stopped, staring at her. "Oh, boy, Ma! *That's it!*" I was pointing at her, my finger moving back and forth like a jackhammer while I laughed like a nut at my newest brilliant idea.

"Oh, no, Danny, how would I dare!" she said, gasping, her face pink. "Besides, I have a date."

"That's just for dinner. You could go to a fast-food place and then come over to the concert. It'll be fun—and you wanted to go anyway. Remember you kept saying how you always wanted to do this, and how lucky Dimples is—"

"Yes, I know, Danny, but this is *different*. I don't even know what music they're doing, and—"

"Oh, you know about everything that's popular. I hear you singing all the time, and you even told me you do it at parties and stuff. . . ."

"Yes, but what about them? Would they want me? I'm not a kid—"

"In an emergency, who cares?"

"I don't know how Wayne would feel about it—"

"I bet he'd love it. Listen, Ma, you never know—there might be some talent scouts there."

"Talent scouts! At a high school disco party?"

I shrugged. "You never know." I headed for the phone. "Should I call Raymond and tell him you'll do it?"

"I—don't know, Danny. Do you really think . . ."

I started dialing Raymond's number. I still had my coat on, but it wasn't so important to get to Tom's house so fast now. "Hello, Raymond? No, I never even got out. Listen, I have some great news for you. I have a singer for tonight. No, I'm not kidding. It's my ma. Why would I be kidding? Sure she will. She's terrific, and she knows about all the songs there are. Didn't you know she's trying to break into show business? You do? Okay, great. Yes, I'll wait right by the phone."

I hung up and smiled at my ma, who had her hands clasped together up over her nose and mouth.

"Raymond thinks it's a terrific idea," I said, grinning at her. "He said he's going to call Chicky with the good news and then call me back with further instructions."

She dropped her hands and let out a long, shaky breath. "Oh, Danny, you're nutty! And I'm nuttier!"

Two seconds later the phone rang and I snapped it up. "She's on!" Raymond screeched. "It's going to be Four Brothers and a Mother. How about *that,* Danny?"

Chapter 5

The music blasted at me and Tom as soon as we got into the building, and by the time we were at my apartment, the walls were vibrating with the electric sound of two guitars and a bass. Inside we heard my ma's clear, pretty voice amplified a hundred times in a really mellow tune:

Tell me, tell me, tell me, do:
You for me and me for you,
Tell me, tell me, tell me whether
You and I can get together.
Tell me, tell me, tell me, *do*-oo,
Tell me, tell me, tell me *true*-oo,
Ooh-oo, *ooh*-oo,
TELL ME!

"Wow," Tom said, "that sounds terrific!"

He and I had driven Raymond and Marcus over to the high school with Marcus's drums and all the electronic equipment except for the stuff they needed here to practice with my ma. Chicky, Lester, and Julian stayed to run through the music with her. They were just finishing the number when we walked into the living room, and my ma waved at us happily. Her eyes were all shiny, and she looked real nice in her silky blue outfit. "Hi," she called, "how did it sound?"

Tom was clapping. "Tremendous!"

I added, "Really great."

"Honest?" she asked, giggling. "We're lucky it's this early, or the neighbors would kill us."

Chicky grinned. "They're just lucky to get a free concert. Okay, now let's go through the last one, and that will be it." He winked at me. "Your mother's a real pro, Danny."

They did another number, and even though the volume was turned way down, my eardrums were humming. They had to stop a few times for my ma to get the words straight, but she picked it up fast, and they told her not to worry, they'd cue her along. Chicky was chewing his gum a mile a minute while his fingers danced along the guitar strings, and Lester, a chubby guy with bangs and longish brown hair, bounced along to the beat of his rhythm guitar, sweating and grinning happily. When I first saw Julian, big and broad and clumsy-looking, I couldn't picture him playing in a rock band, but as I watched his fingers flying over his bass, his body moving gracefully to the rhythm, I was amazed. And then, by some miracle through all that, I heard the bleeping buzz of our doorbell.

The Mustache stood there in the hall with this stunned expression as the blast of music hit him. He was all dressed up in a brown suit and cream-colored shirt and fancy tie, and with his thick, reddish-blond hair and big mustache and his face pink with surprise, he looked like a special gift wrap. I never would have recognized him out of uniform.

"Hi," I said, "come on in. Don't mind the noise —we're having a little jam session."

"Oh," and he gave a funny laugh, "I was wondering why you'd have the stereo up so high. You've got some pretty talented friends, Danny." I could see he was a lot more relaxed already. I nodded toward the living room. "Come on in, my ma's inside."

"Who's the singer?" he asked as he followed me. "She sounded pretty good."

"Wayne!" my ma cried when she saw him. "When did you get here?"

He was smiling now and not nearly as pink. "Just now—in time to hear the last line of that song. Who was singing, anyway?" He looked around at the guys, who just stood there grinning at him. They all knew the whole story about the date. "Hey, what's going on, Laura? Who are these guys, anyway?" His eyes bored a hole through her now: "Was that *you* singing?"

Now her face got pink. "As a matter of fact, it was. Listen, Wayne, would you mind if we changed our plans a little?"

All the guys started getting their stuff together while my ma and Wayne went into the kitchen to talk.

"What if he doesn't go for it?" Julian said as he snapped his guitar case shut.

"Shh," Tom warned him, "he will. Why wouldn't he? He looks like a nice guy."

Lester shrugged. "Well, you never know. Maybe he hates music."

"Maybe he hates kids," Julian put in.

"Ha, that's all I'd need!" Chicky hissed. "First the chicken pox, then a welsher."

"A what?" I said.

Tom laughed. "Never mind. Listen, you guys, I guarantee you, you don't have to worry. If he was that kind of guy, Danny's mom wouldn't be interested in him."

"Well," Chicky said, "all I know is we better get moving. I hope they come out soon with the verdict."

Lester was looking at his watch. "Yeah, and I hope they're fast eaters."

"Okay, everything's cool."

We looked up to see my ma and Wayne standing in the doorway, smiling as she said, "Wayne's a really good sport. We're going to that little neighborhood place for a quick bite—I'm too nervous to eat, anyway."

"We can go somewhere nice afterwards, then," he said, "while we wait for the reviews to come out."

"Hey, he really *is* a nice guy," Julian said as we finished packing the van and started out for the high school. "I guess your mom knows how to pick 'em, Danny."

I smiled. "She couldn't have done it without me." I was in the seat next to Tom, and he reached over and patted me on the shoulder.

Chicky, Julian, and Lester carried in their instruments, Tom took the amp and mike, and I brought the rest of the tools and patch cords. After Chicky showed the security guard at the school his authorization, he nodded, smiling at everyone, until his eyes fell on me, bringing up the rear.

"Who're you, kid?"

"I'm with the group." The rest of them were walking on, yacking away with each other and not even noticing.

He pointed at them as they were quickly disappearing down the corridor. *"You* with *them?* You're too young to be here. What's in that box?"

"It's the rest of our tools—hey, you guys!" I called, but Lester, walking behind all of them, was just disappearing around the corner.

"Can I go get them? They don't even know—"

He was reaching for the toolbox. "Never mind, let me just take a look." He snapped open the clasps and saw the tangle of tools, then looked at the circle of wire over my arm. I was looking at the shiny buttons of his uniform and the walkie-talkie strapped to his belt that was almost at my eye level. He closed the box, put it on the floor between his feet, and picked up his walkie-talkie. "Four-three-oh, four-three-oh, over. Yeah, Mike here at the main entrance. Those musician guys get to the gym yet? Send the head guy back here." He snapped it back on his belt. "How old are you anyway, kid?"

Now I was really starting to get nervous. Should

I lie about my age so he'd let me in? But what age was I supposed to *be* to get in? Not less than fifteen to be in high school, I figured. But then . . .

"Hey, fella," he prompted. He had his arms crossed over his chest now, but there was a sort of smile, just at the corners of his mouth.

"I'm small for my age," I began. And then Chicky appeared.

"Danny, what happened to you, anyway? We didn't even know you weren't . . . oh-oh!" Chewing madly on his gum he sputtered at the guard, "Listen, he's part of our group, man. A kid brother, *you* know. We're the Four Brothers and a—hey, remember I showed you that permit? Well, he's another brother—a kid brother." He looked at the cable on my arm, then spotted the toolbox on the floor. "Oh, hey, man, you didn't think this squirt had burglar tools, did you?"

The guard burst out laughing and bent down to pick up the toolbox. "No, I didn't. I was just wondering why you lunks wandered off leaving your kid brother here." He handed me the box and squeezed my shoulder; it felt like he took a piece off. "Say, you never did tell me how old you are."

I laughed, grabbing the box. "Twelve."

He had a big smile as he gave each of us a shove toward the gym. "Get going, fellas. And listen—take better care of your kid brother, hear?"

The gym was echoing with all kinds of wild activity. High school kids were setting up tables and chairs in half-circle rows, others were decorating the walls, some were testing out blinking lights. Chicky was all full of the story about me and the guard. I walked away, embarrassed, and started fooling with the stuff they had piled in a corner.

"Hey, Danny, come here!" Raymond had a big smirk. "Why didn't you just tell that security guy you're our mascot?" They all laughed real loud, and I did, too, but Julian shook his head. "What do you mean, Raymond? He's our kid brother!" Lester came over and put his arm around my shoulder. "Yeah, the kind every guy dreams of having—only around when you want him."

"For a little while there, I had the feeling you didn't want me around," I said, and they all hooted.

"Okay, enough recreation," Chicky ordered, "let's get to work. Danny, where's the mike?"

We all sprang into action, working together to finish setting up. Raymond and Marcus had done all the big things before we came, but now they had to check the details, connect the mikes, test the sound, and tune their instruments. Some of the other kids came over to see what we were doing and helped Raymond test the lighting. Every couple of minutes someone called me to get a pliers or bring some tape or tacks or wire, and by the time everything was all finished, I felt like one of the most important people in the world. All of a sudden, from being this new kid in a great big city who didn't know a single person, here I was being everyone's kid brother and a real rock group's general handyman. Not to mention the son of the beautiful vocalist who was walking in now with Wayne, looking like the star of the whole scene.

"How did you get in?" I asked them.

Wayne nodded at my ma. "She told the man she's your mother."

They all liked that but me; I was trying to figure out if they were poking fun.

"Danny," my ma said after they finished tuning up and the high school kids started piling into the gym, "I want you and Wayne to sit over there"—she pointed at a table all the way on the side, near the band—"so I can see you whenever I need to."

Well, she needed to pretty much at the beginning. My face started aching from forcing those big, encouraging smiles, but Wayne looked like it was real easy for him. No wonder—she was great!

The kids loved it. They went wild when Chicky announced right at the beginning: "We have a little change in our group tonight—the Sister came down with chicken pox, so tonight we're the Four Brothers and a Mother. I give you—" and he turned to the band and introduced each musician, then swept his arm out toward my ma as he said, "And Laura Turner, the Mother!"

The kids went wild, shrieking and clapping and making comments like, "She could be my mother anytime!" and Wayne and I exchanged secret smiles.

The concert was a smash. Raymond and Tom came over and sat with us when they saw everything was working okay and helped out with the big smiles for my ma; but after a while she didn't even need them anymore because her audience was giving her all the courage she could ever want. The guys were helping her out with the words, too; and even though she was real nervous at the beginning, she got over it pretty soon and started walking around with the mike and doing those dance movements that a lot of singers do. The whole disco setup with the blinking lights and different colors and the music, loud but sounding really great, and the kids dancing and grooving on it—well, it was more like a dream or a movie than something that was really happening.

"Danny, want a hot dog and some cold pop?" Wayne asked me later.

"Thanks," I said, "I sure would. Uh, maybe you'd better not let my ma know, though. She's on a health-food kick."

But my ma didn't care what I ate that night, she was so deep into the excitement of what she was doing. And the way everyone clapped for her, she could hardly come back down to earth.

Poor Wayne—for his first date with Ma, he sure had to put up with a lot. But he looked as if he was having pretty much fun, just the way I was. I liked being with him, too. He was so relaxed and didn't talk unless he felt like it and seemed interested in anything I told him. Not that we could do much talking in all that noise.

It was fun watching the kids dance, too; and when some girls came over to talk to Raymond and Tom, Wayne kept muttering, "Ask them to dance, dummies, that's what they're here for." Tom finally did, and we cheered him on with secret little signals that would crack him up. But Raymond just sat there talking to one girl and another about all this technical stuff until their eyes would about glaze over with boredom and they'd slink away back to their friends. Finally Wayne said, "Why don't you get out there and dance, Raymond? Those girls don't want to hear about amps and resistors—they just want to jump around and have fun like all the other kids."

Raymond sort of hunched into himself. "I'm not interested in dancing." He dropped his head just the littlest bit. "Besides, I don't know how."

Wayne shrugged. "This kind of dancing, there's nothing to know—you just bounce around in time to the music. See? The way Tom is." He laughed then. "Look who's talking—the one with two left feet. Hey, what can I get you guys to drink?"

After my ma's last number, three men and two women came over to our table to talk to her. They were parents and teachers there to supervise the evening, and they gave her compliments about her singing and then started asking her how come she was doing it. She explained about Dimples and the chickenpox, and they shook their heads in wonder.

"You've got a lot of talent," one of the women said, "Have you thought about doing this professionally?"

My ma looked at me and I looked at her, and we both burst out laughing.

The other woman shook her head and smiled. "Well, I guess you have." She turned to the man beside her. "Andy, what about Gus?"

He shrugged, reached into his back pocket, and took out his wallet. "Here," he said, pulling a card from inside it, "my brother manages singers, groups. You can call him and use my name if you want, Andy Jacoby. Tell him I said I'd bet on you."

Wayne wrote the guy's name on the back of the card and put it in my ma's bag, because she was too shaky by then to do anything. All the guys were crowded around her now, telling her how great she was, and she hugged them, then grabbed me and just about squeezed all my breath away. "This is my good luck charm!" she said, reaching for my face, but I pulled away just in time to dodge the kiss she had ready, and they all started yelling, "Hey, I'll take it!"

"Listen," she said, "I want all of you to come over on Sunday for supper. We'll have a big celebration then."

"Should we bring our instruments?" Julian asked.

"Yeah, we can jam!" Lester cried.

"Well, I don't know," my ma answered, looking at me. "What do you think, Danny? The neighbors . . ."

I shrugged. "We have pretty thick walls."

"No, I think not," she said. "Not on a Sunday. Let's break them in gently."

When she and Wayne left, Raymond and Tom told her they would stay with me till she came home. "Oh, you don't have to do that," she said.

"That's okay," Tom said, "we can watch some TV. After all," and he winked at me, "what are big brothers for?"

Chapter 6

Did you ever hear of "sibling rivalry"? It's a fancy term for being jealous of your sisters or brothers. Well, I must be the only kid in history who suffered from it without having any sisters or brothers.

It started that next day when Tom and I went to the auto show up at Navy Pier. At least it was supposed to be Tom and I, but as we were walking over to the bus stop, he said, "Raymond's supposed to meet us here—hey, there he is!" I had this funny feeling when I saw Raymond starting to run toward us in his clumsy, cloddy way: glad to see the person I liked and admired so much, but a little disappointed that I wouldn't have Tom all to myself that day. Just feeling that way surprised me, like a big sneeze coming on that you never even knew was there. I wondered if it was because I was afraid I wouldn't make as much headway in my "research" for becoming a Renaissance Man—or if I was just plain afraid that they would be more interested in each other than they were in me. Or both.

"How's the kid brother?" Raymond said, bending over to grab at my elbow. "Hey, look at that sky

—do you think it's going to snow today?" He made a loud shuddering noise. "It sure feels like it!"

"Snow!" I yelped. "It's only October."

"Yes, my young man, but you forget, this is Chicago."

"Is that true?" I asked Tom. "Does it really snow here in October?"

He laughed. "Don't you know by now that everything Raymond says is true?"

I looked from one to the other as it dawned on me that the day before yesterday they didn't even know each other, and now here they were acting like best buddies. I mean, they met through me and practically overnight had become better friends than . . . I shook my head as if to stop those stupid thoughts.

Raymond was looking at me seriously now. "Trust me, Danny. It might snow today."

They both howled with laughter, but all I could do was force a weak smile. I still didn't know if they were just fooling around with me or if they really meant it. And I got that funny feeling of being the extra person—the fifth wheel on the wagon. It kept on like that, from the bus ride when they pushed me into the only empty seat and stood by, talking to each other, until they found a seat together farther back. And again on the second bus that we had to transfer to.

This time we all sat together in the back, with me in the middle. They were talking about cars with diesel engines being better or worse than cars with regular gas engines, and it was pretty interesting, even though I didn't know anything about it. Each time one made a point that sounded like a winner, I'd side with him till the other would come up with an opposite argument that sounded just as good, and I'd switch. Raymond was saying how diesel is better than gas because you get so much more efficiency, and Tom was arguing that it didn't pay for what you lost out on in performance. He said even the difference in price wasn't worth it anymore, and Raymond insisted he was wrong and that you had to have a "diesel mentality" to be able to appreciate its advantages. "It's the guys who have to patch out at every stoplight who bad-mouth the diesel engines," Raymond told him. "In the long run the diesels do much better in mpg."

"What's that?" I asked.

"Miles per gallon."

I nodded. "Oh, yeah."

I was learning, all right, and after we got inside the show, they both kept turning around to explain things to me. And whenever I had a question they'd both jump in to give me the answer. But more of the time they'd talk together about the technical parts of the exhibits while I just listened and looked at everything in sight, gawking at all the fascinating things on display.

There were tons of new cars and gadgets and special equipment in every kind of display you can imagine, from women with loads of make-up dressed in real fancy clothes standing next to or sitting on cars on rotating stands, to big displays of car telephones and intercoms, to little booths where someone sat at a card table trying to interest people in some new energy-saving gimmick to install in their cars. Raymond got all excited when we came to the exhibit on electronic controls.

"Tom, look at that set-up!" He pointed to the computerized dashboard that had all kinds of indicators lit up. "It's microprocessors. They diagnose the problems." He started asking the man in charge questions, then turned to us and explained: "See, they can be programmed to make automatic engine adjustments—like the proper air-fuel mixture and then that would automatically adjust the spark timing and exhaust-gas recirculation."

At the next display, Tom turned to me: "Look at that digital speedometer, Danny. Think we could put one of those in my limo? Oh, hey, man, will you look at *this!*" He was pulling at Raymond's arm excitedly, putting his fingers to his lips. "Shh, listen." A funny voice was coming out of this little black gadget on the dashboard saying: "Please turn off your lights."

"Can you believe it?" Tom cried.

Raymond nodded, smiling wisely. "A voice synthesizer. I read about those. Not bad."

They laughed when I added, "Pretty polite. It even says 'please'."

That's when we got to my favorite—the Great Cars Exhibit. It's funny, Tom was the big car man, but Raymond was the walking encyclopedia. As usual. There wasn't a car he hadn't heard of. Tom was amazed.

"How do you know all this stuff, anyway?" Tom asked him.

Raymond shrugged. "Oh, I pick it up here and there . . ."

Tom shook his head in astonishment. "I could understand it if you had your nose in a book all the time, but from what I've seen of you already, you don't look like you spend that much time in one place."

Raymond laughed. "You're right about that. Actually, I do pick up a lot from reading, but I kind of poke my nose into everything I can and ask a lot of questions about the things that interest me."

Tom stopped and fixed him with a real hard look. "Is there anything you're *not* interested in?"

Just as serious Raymond answered, "There must be plenty of things, but I can't think of any at the moment. Oh, hey, look at *this* neat little number!"

It was a 1936 Ford Cabriolet, and it was some kind of a beautiful car, let me tell you. We all stood there grooving on it, and Raymond said, "Listen, man, you better feast your eyes on these special jobs here so we can do some fancy work on your machine."

"All right, man, all right, all right," Tom jabbered, practically in a trance. I wondered if they'd have any time for me once they got into working together on Tom's car. The most I could do was be their hand-me man: hand me this and hand me that. My dreams of Little Brotherhood were fading away almost as fast as my dreams of becoming a Renaissance Man. Maybe, I figured, I ought to think about switching careers to a Friendship Service—introducing people to each other so they could become friends. Something like a dating service. Yeah—I'd heard about Computer Dating. This could be Computer Friendships for Lonely Teenagers. Not that Tom and Raymond were lonely, but . . . I looked at them, talking so eagerly together now about the Buick Phaeton, another classic car beauty, and wondered if they would ever have become friends if they'd met each other on their own instead of through me.

On the bus ride back Tom said almost those same words. We were all sitting together in the back, our shopping bags that they gave out at the show crammed full of the pamphlets and ads and booklets from the exhibits. "Raymond, if you and I met somewhere we'd probably never had said more than hi."

Raymond nodded. "Yep, that's true. This kid here really gets things going, doesn't he?"

They both looked at me with such warm, nice smiles, I tried not to think of how Raymond had picked up me and my ma at the museum the other week. He may have been the one to get things going for a start, but I wasn't so bad at jumping in and keeping them moving.

"Don't forget about tomorrow," I reminded

them as we got off the second bus. "Three o'clock at my house."

"Are you kidding?" Raymond cried. "I'm not eating anything till then—tell your mom to make twice as much as she was planning."

I laughed, then suddenly looked up at the sky, which was darkening now. There was an even deeper chill in the air, and the clouds made long, purplish streaks against the setting orange sun. "Hey, Raymond, what about the snow?"

He shrugged. "Look at that—I was wrong!"

Tom laughed. "It just shows you, Danny—you can't trust anyone anymore. Not even Raymond."

"Well, I'll give you both another chance," I said, and suddenly they each rushed at me and boosted me way up in the air, making a seat of their hands, and started running a little as they yelled stuff like, "That's our kid, Danny!" and "He's the greatest!" Let me tell you, I felt like a king!

"I have a surprise for you," my ma said the next day while we were getting the house ready for company. "I decided that one day out of every weekend will be Culture Day for us."

"*Culture* Day! What's that?"

She laughed. "You know, doing cultural things—going to the theater and the ballet and concerts. . . ."

"Hey, Ma, I hope you didn't get carried away by that Renaissance Man idea. That's one thing, but culture is another. Ballet and *symphonies* and stuff? Oh, *Ma!*"

"I really meant more like going to see shows and on sightseeing trips and—well, things that you can learn a lot from and have fun while you're doing them. After all, we have to work our way into this thing gradually."

"Yeah," I grunted, going for the dustmop.

She shrugged. "I can see that my idea really turns you on. Well, what about if I told you I got us tickets to see *Rainbow* for next Saturday afternoon?"

"What is it?"

Her smile vanished. "What *is* it? Only the biggest hit show of the year, that's all! It just opened last week, and they're sold out for three months. Someone at work got extra tickets and offered to sell them to me first, so I grabbed them. In fact, that's what gave me the idea for our Culture Days. I figured we would plan something for one day every weekend—that would leave each of us a day free to do things with our own friends. And sometimes we could include them, too. Except for very expensive things, like these tickets."

"Sounds fine to me. What's this show about, anyway?"

"It's a musical, about a kid your age, as a matter of fact, who has all kinds of adventures while he takes a trip around the world."

"Alone?"

"I'm not sure, Danny, but it got rave reviews, and it sounded like something you would like."

When I saw her hurt look, I realized I'd better soften up. "Well, that's real nice, Ma. Thank you. Hey, remember in New York you used to take me to those little-kid shows a lot?"

She nodded. "Sure. You loved it. Remember the time we went to that play about pirates, and you ran up and wanted to pick up the sword when the actor dropped it?"

I laughed, remembering how she had tried to stop me but when the actor saw me he beckoned me to come on and do it. It wasn't a real stage—the play was in a church basement, and I was so fascinated by it I just went on up to be part of it. "And remember those shows where the people had paper bags for costumes?" I added.

"Oh, Danny, they were marvelous! You used to want to go to see them all the time."

"Yeah. We did so many fun things in New York."

"And we can do just as much here. There's always a lot going on in Chicago, Danny. Right now I have a list so long we'd have to live here forever if we wanted to do it all."

"Do you think we will, Ma?"

"What—live here forever or do it all?"

I laughed. "I don't know. Both, I guess."

She leaned over and put both her hands on my shoulders, looking me in the eyes. "Who knows where Fate will take us, Danny? Maybe tomorrow something will happen that will completely change our lives."

"Like what?" I said. It had already happened once.

She threw up her hands and flung her head back and forth as she said, "Oh, Danny, how do I know?" Then she bent over and pinched my cheek real hard, grinning. "We'll just have to wait and see is all."

When the guys started trouping in, in a little while, I kept thinking how I wasn't so sure I would want Fate to move me anywhere else. Not for a while, at least, not while I was having such a good time with this all-of-a-sudden family of big brothers who thought I was such hot stuff.

Bones and Raymond were the first to come. Bones brought a lentil loaf his sister had made, and Raymond's stepmother sent a big batch of biscuits. My ma and I were really surprised, because everyone walked in with something. Chicky brought a bowl of fruit, Marcus a casserole of Chinese vegetables, Julian a pan of brownies, Lester an apple cake, and Tom a basket of cheeses.

Wayne got there last, still in uniform because he came straight from work, but he brought a change of clothes and a big jar of white clam sauce. "His specialty," my ma explained. She had made a bean salad and artichoke spaghetti.

"*What* kind?" I said when she set the bowl on the table. It looked like regular spaghetti to me, but she shook her finger at me. "Now don't be prejudiced, Danny, just because it's healthy. It's much better for you, has more protein and less starch, and you don't feel like a bag of cement after you've eaten a ton of it." She laughed. "I spent practically all my salary on it, so you see how serious I am about keeping you all in good condition."

Well, let me tell you, we had some feast! Wayne and my ma had planned on his making the sauce, but she wasn't expecting anyone else to bring anything. She also didn't expect the kind of eating they were all able to do! "Heavens," she said as the dishes started getting empty, "is this how you're going to eat when you're their age, Danny?" and they all roared.

Chicky gave her one of his funny, crooked smiles. "You better start getting used to it, Mother." After the concert they had all started calling her "The Mother," and now everyone laughed when he said that. There were too many of us to sit around the table, so we had set all the food out on it and helped ourselves and were sitting in the living room, a lot of us on the floor, picnic style.

The food was fantastic, and everyone kidded Wayne about his clam sauce. "It's the only thing I know how to make," he said. There were about five different conversations going on at once, and people kept hopping up to go for seconds and thirds. My ma was right about the spaghetti—you could eat a lot of it without feeling weighted down, but it tasted like regular spaghetti. The lentil loaf was awful, but even that went. The stereo was on low, and with the room all filled with people and talk, it was like one of those party scenes you see in the movies.

Bones told me he was going to come over after

wrestling practice to give me some coaching and said I should pick a day, and then Chicky asked me, "Did you ever have the chicken pox?" When I told him yes, he said, "That's good, because I think Dimples is still contagious. You can come to my house—we have two acoustic guitars we can use. I'd rather start you on that. When do you want your first lesson?"

Tom and Raymond were talking about scouting some junkyards for car parts and asked if I'd come along. That booked me up for Monday, Wednesday, and Friday.

"It sounds like an awfully busy week," my ma said. "Are you sure you can handle it, Danny—and your schoolwork?"

"Don't worry, Mother," Tom said, "we'll make sure he does it all. Right, little brother?"

Wayne laughed. The guys all liked him and asked him about his work and his adventures on the police force. He told them how between the interesting hair-raisers there was mostly hard work and a lot of boring detail, but how you always had to be ready for the something big that might happen the next minute.

I thought about that after everyone left. In a way, what Wayne said described my life, too. Even an ordinary day of going to school often turned out to be a time when something special happened. As for right now, I had my work cut out for me: to get to be as smart as Raymond, as talented as Chicky, as strong as Bones, and as cool as Tom. It just showed, having a good attitude and the right luck, your everyday life could be an adventure. I had no way of knowing that the biggest adventure of my life was waiting for me on one of those ordinary days.

Chapter 7

Maybe it's because I started feeling more relaxed about living in Chicago and getting used to the new school and all, but when I went back to school that next week, things were different. For the first time I had this real comfortable feeling, like I belonged there. Guys started asking me to sit with them at lunch; and before I knew it, they were interested in finding out about me and what it was like to live in New York and all. It was as if something clicked and I was switched from being an outsider to one of the regulars. A few of the guys even asked me to do special things with them after school, and I wanted to say yes because I liked all of them. But wouldn't you know—it was on the three days I was booked with Big Brothers! I told each of the guys I had something else on that I would try to switch; and by changing my guitar session with Chicky I managed to go to a photography workshop with Mitsu and I worked it out to play basketball with Adam and his friends on Thursday. I told Rupert, who had asked if I just wanted to hang out with him on Wednesday, that I didn't have any time that week but I'd like to the next week. I had every day filled, and even my ma was real happy about it because she knew where I was and what I was doing all the time.

"As long as you're home by suppertime and keep up with your schoolwork," she told me, adding, "Besides, Danny, it's important for you to have friends your own age. When you get to know them better, we can invite them on our Culture Days."

Inside I groaned, but I just said, "Yeah, that's a great idea, Ma."

Well, it sure was a busy week. My first guitar lesson was fun, and I was surprised that Chicky could be such a patient teacher. He really loved his music, and we went over reading notes and checking out the guitar and how to tune it, and he showed me two chords. I was using his acoustic guitar, and he was using his sister's; and he told me that after the next lesson, he'd let me take his home to practice on.

I got a fast look at Dimples when I came, but she ran upstairs because she didn't want me to see her chicken pox. "Was she mad because my ma took her place?" I whispered.

Chicky laughed. "No, but she wouldn't like it if it happened when she wasn't sick."

Bones gave me a heavy workout, starting me on a routine of exercises and teaching me some of the basic wrestling holds. It was fun, and he told me I could be good if I tried hard, but that I had to work out regularly. "You ought to start running, too, Danny," he told me. "Ask your mother to get you a good pair of running shoes for Christmas." Then he added, "But it would be much better if you could have them now, because once winter sets in. . . ." He shrugged and laughed, but I shivered.

I kept hearing about how awful the winters were in Chicago, and when I'd ask, "Are they really that bad?" half the people would say, "Just wait and see!" and the other half, "No, people exaggerate—winter is winter. In Chicago it's just a little more so."

"It's not as bad as Minnesota or North Dakota," Wayne told us that other night, and all the guys had laughed and joked. "Yeah, it's like a Caribbean Island." And then Wayne laughed, too, and said, "Have you heard about our summers?"

"They can't be worse than New York," my ma told him, and Raymond quipped, "Want to bet?"

But I figured since there were millions of people who lived here and they all survived, how bad could it be? Besides, there were some things about Chicago I liked even better than New York. It was cleaner and had a sort of homey feeling, and I liked seeing trees and green stuff right in the downtown section. But what I liked most of all was the way people were so friendly. Even though it's one of the biggest cities in the United States, I started feeling right at home from the start, and my ma did, too.

Anyway, I was trying to figure out how to ask her for running shoes, since she had just bought me a pair of expensive sneakers. "They're for basketball and sports like that," Bones told me when he saw them, "but you'll harm your feet if you run in the wrong shoes." I had decided to wait till Saturday to bring up the subject.

Then Saturday came and we had to stop at the neighborhood bank to cash my ma's paycheck before we went downtown for lunch in one of the fancy hotels—that was to be part of our Culture Days, too. She figured we would have enough time to make the show and do all that if we skipped breakfast, because we got up late, so I decided to ask her at lunch. But we never made it that far.

Even though the day was sunny and bright, it was pretty nippy out.

"Look, aren't they cute!" My ma pointed at a bunch of little kids in those dumb costumes you buy in packages. "Don't tell me Halloween is today, and we won't be home for Trick or Treat!" She had stopped dead, looking all horrified.

I laughed. "No, Ma, it's tomorrow—they're just trying to get some extra mileage out of it!"

Now she laughed, too. "Oh, Danny, you're so cynical! You probably did the same thing when you were their age."

"Yeah, except I would never wear those yucky costumes—they all look alike. Remember the great ones you and Aunt Dorothy used to make me?"

Her eyes got all soft. "Yes, remember, Danny? That scarecrow, and the robot, when we used the cardboard from dress boxes and covered it with all that tinfoil?"

"And I couldn't bend my legs?" We were both laughing now.

She shook her head. "I think we had more fun

making them for you than you had wearing them! Oh, she called last night after you were asleep, I forgot to tell you."

"Aunt Dorothy?"

She nodded.

"Why?"

"Just to talk. She misses us. She sends you her love."

"Why doesn't she come to visit? She promised she would when we left New York."

She laughed again. "We haven't been gone that long, Danny! Anyway, I told her she should plan on coming for Christmas. And I told her about the concert and all your substitute brothers and about that agent and how interested he is—oooh, Danny, did I forget to tell you that, too?"

I guess it was the look on my face that stopped her.

"WHAT agent?"

"You know—the one who's the brother of that teacher—"

"*Oh,* at the concert. The one who gave you his card. You called him?"

"Yesterday. He said he'd like to hear me." She hit her forehead. "I can't believe I forgot to tell you! I need to call Chicky and see if I can get together with the group. He said he'll listen to me sing if I can arrange to get some time to see him."

"Oh, Ma, wow, that's great! How could you forget such an important thing?"

"I didn't forget—I remembered to tell Aunt

Dorothy, didn't I? I'll call Chicky tomorrow." She laughed. "He said he's not interested in teenage rock groups, but I could bring the others if I'd feel more comfortable with them as background." We were at the bank. "I hope it won't take too long in here. I'm starving."

"Me too." I looked through the big glass doors. "It doesn't look too crowded," I said.

"Not for a Saturday morning anyway."

She got in the shortest line, around five people. The guy ahead of her was wearing jeans with big holes that reminded me of the Halloween I dressed like a hippie. My ma and I had taken my most raggedy jeans and cut funny-shaped holes all over. I wondered if he was dressing up for Halloween, too, or if he was just a poor college student. He had a black wool cap pulled down over his ears and one of those green hooded jackets with the bright orange lining. I knew it was because the jacket was all dirty that my ma stood back a little, just the way I knew exactly what she was thinking as she looked over at the other two, longer lines.

"Ah-ah-ah," I warned, "remember what you always say about changing lines!"

"It never pays," she agreed, laughing that tinkly laugh that always makes people turn around to look. When this guy in front of her did, I was surprised at how old he looked, like around thirty. You couldn't see much of his pasty-white face for the scruffy brown beard, but he had a pair of green eyes that bored holes right through you. The line moved up, and my ma shrugged and took her paycheck out of her handbag.

"I'll wait over there," I told her, nodding at the wall filled with paintings. The biggest one had the same face painted all over it in neat rows, each one a different color. The background was black, and the face was the kind a little kid draws. But the colors were so deep and bright—red and purple and green and orange, every color—it got me really fascinated. Underneath was a little white card: "DIFFERENT FACES, Jeffrey Kalucki, Age 10." The next painting was smaller—a barn with two horses, a fence, and grass—and looked like a picture in a magazine. The card underneath said: "THE FARM, Susan Kaplan, Age 11." *Wow,* I thought, *these kids are really on their way!*

At first I didn't pay any attention to the commotion behind me. But when I finally turned around to see how my ma was doing, I couldn't believe my eyes. This guy who had been in front of her in line was standing by the teller's counter with a gun. A GUN! And he was turned around toward everyone in the bank now, holding up the gun. The commotion I had heard was gasps of surprise as the whole thing was happening, right behind my back! But I hadn't missed much.

"Now, don't anyone move, y'hear? This is a holdup." I wasn't sure of the next sound—almost like a laugh—as he added: "In case you didn't know."

Boy, I thought, *a wisecracking bank robber!*

"Like, be cool, folks, and no one gets hurt, okay?"

"No, it's *not* okay!" chirped this little skinny woman with white hair.

He took a step, aiming his gun right at her, and the old man next to her clapped his hand over her mouth. Someone screamed, and the gunman spun around. I took a step toward my ma, but she gave me such a hard look, I stopped. She looked sort of funny, standing there clutching her paycheck. I sneaked a look around to see what the security guard was doing. There wasn't any. By now it was so quiet, all you could hear was the bank teller stuffing money into a big plastic shopping bag. And everyone's nervous breathing.

The holdup guy was still glaring at the old woman, and she had her lips all pinched in and was glaring right back at him. Suddenly he let out a hoot of laughter. "Hey, you're a spunky little old one, all right. You remind me of my grammaw." He waved the gun at her. "Just don't go too far, y'hear?" He spun around again, addressing everyone now. "All of you!" He sidled over to the teller's counter, his bright eyes darting everywhere. The teller pushed the brown plastic shopping bag toward him, and as he started picking it up I noticed all the people in back looking outside. There, through the big glass doors, was what looked like a sea of blue-black uniforms. Wow—just like in the movies: the cops had come, right in the nick of time!

As they swarmed toward the doors, Mr. Holey

Jeans turned, gun still cocked in one hand and shopping bag clutched in the other. The moment he saw the cops, he dropped the bag and started running, right toward my ma. I headed over to her from the other side, and we both reached her in the same instant, me grabbing her around the waist and he grabbing the both of us, holding us together in a stranglehold as he screamed at the cops, "Freeze or I kill them both!" They were halfway in the door by then, and there were gasps and muffled screams. But what I heard the loudest was my heart thumping, and what I felt the strongest was that bony arm and my ma's bony shoulder. He had us pinned against him with his left arm, while with his right hand he held his shiny black gun two inches from my ma's ear.

The cops froze, their hands up.

"Outside!" He wasn't wisecracking any more. "Hold it!" he called as they were going. "Leave one of your walkie-talkies on the floor." After they were all out, he nodded at the little white-haired woman. "Okay, Grammaw, go get that thing and bring it here. You're going to be my secretary." Finally he loosened his grip around me and my ma, but he was still hanging on. Both of us were shaking so much, it took a while before I realized he was shaking, too.

"You know how to work this thing?" he asked the woman when she came back with the two-way radio.

She shook her head no. "I do!" I said.

"Yeah?" He looked down at me, then let go his

hold on me and my ma but still kept the gun near her face. "Well, then, let's get to work, hero. First find out if they can hear us okay."

They heard us okay. There was this creepy silence inside the bank, so when their message came through it echoed. "Why don't you just put down your gun," the cop said. "Come out peacefully, and no one will get hurt."

"Tell 'em no dice!" he said to me. "I went through all this; I'm not going to blow it now, man."

"He said no dice," I began, feeling like the anchor man on the evening news. "He said—"

"Hey," he cut in, "never mind, kid. Just hold it up and press the right buttons. I'll do the talking."

"Okay." I shrugged, holding the radio up for him. "It's on." It was a nice job while it lasted, I thought, then saw a bunch of police cars pulling up outside, some with quick blasts of sirens that stopped short.

"Listen," he was telling them now, "if you don't pull any funny stuff, I'll send you all your people out nice and cool."

My ma and I looked at each other and had to bite our lips to keep from ya-hooing.

"We give you our word," they said.

I was so happy, he had to poke me to remind me to press the button for him to answer, and I jumped, almost dropping the darn thing.

"Except for the kid and his mother," he announced. "They stay."

"Why?" came the voice back. "Why don't you let them go, too?"

"They're my hostages."

My ma turned white, and I started feeling real weak.

"Let's talk about it," they said.

They talked about it, but nothing would change his mind. You could see the cops were all milling around out there; there were four of them clustered around the radio, and all the rest were standing back against the crowds that were forming or just keeping an eye on things.

He let everyone go out, except me and my ma. And he never moved that gun away. All the time, I felt sort of numb, like it wasn't really happening to me. Like it was a dream that I would wake up from the next minute.

A lot of the people looked at us before they left, as if they wanted to say something, but no one did because of the icy green stare they were getting. Except for the little white-haired lady. She stopped when she got to the door, turned around, and said, "Now don't you hurt them!"

"Get going, Grammaw," he snapped, pointing the gun at her, and she hurried out, sniffing like you do when you try not to answer back.

"Do you think we could sit down?" my ma asked in this tiny voice. "I feel so weak."

I was worried about her. She looked awful, real pale and tired. I was feeling pretty rotten myself.

"Sure," he said, pointing at the chairs in the

little lounge area. "I don't want you fainting on me or anything like that."

She had hold of my hand real tight—hers was like ice—as we walked over to the chairs; she pushed me down into the first one and then sat beside me. He followed us, one eye on the outside, still holding his trusty gun up, but not close now. "You see," she told him as he sat right across from us where he could watch the door, "we haven't had anything at all to eat today. There wasn't any time—"

"Oh, hey, that's a good idea—let's order some food!" He reached out his hand to me. "Bring me that thing, I'll take it over now."

I gave him the walkie-talkie, and flipping it on, he said: "Could you send in some food?" He covered the speaker, the way you do when you're talking on the phone, and asked us: "What should we order?"

I just looked at my ma, because I knew if I opened my mouth I'd crack up laughing. It was as if we were in a restaurant, for Pete's sake, instead of holed up in a bank after a stickup. My ma shrugged. "Anything's okay with us. I mean, I'm a vegetarian, but I don't really care right now. . . ."

"Hey," our gunman said, "what do you know—so am I!" He removed his hand and talked into the speaker: "Could you send in some veggie stuff—Chinese would be good. Not too spicy." He looked at us. "We don't want us getting too thirsty."

"We'll get it for you right away," they answered. "Then after you've eaten and rested some, we can get all straightened out, okay?"

"We'll see," he answered, leaning back. It was the first time he looked anywhere near relaxed, but he still held the gun up. "Hey, don't forget the fortune cookies."

"Sure," came the reply. "Say, what's your name, fella?"

"Simon," he replied.

"Simon what?"

"Just Simon."

"What about the other two? What are their names?"

He looked at us, and when my ma told him, he said, "Her name's Laura Turner and her kid is Danny."

"Fine, okay, Simon. Now, while you're waiting for the food, how about telling us what you have in mind."

"Well, I'm going to have to give that a little thought. Just don't try anything, because like you can see, I have my gun ready. And I'm not just coming out and giving up, man, so if you have that in your head, forget it. I have this pretty lady in here and this kid, and I know none of you would want them to get hurt, so just be cool, Jack. I'm getting out of here with what I came in for, and I want to go somewhere safe where I can use it and enjoy it. I was always peaceful—man, I'm from the peace generation. But it never got me anywhere, so I'm trying a better way. Let's have the chow and then we'll talk business." He released the talk button, and in a little while a great big brown bag filled with a whole bunch of white food cartons was pushed through the bank door. After the door closed, Simon told me to go get the bag.

"Hey, Danny," he called after I started, and when I turned around he pointed at the gun. "Don't try any funny stuff, okay?"

"Okay." When I picked up the bag, all those good smells hit me, and I wondered if I was feeling so weak from being hungry or being scared. I decided it was both.

Chapter 8

They even remembered to send us plates and forks and napkins. And there was a whole big bagful of fortune cookies.

The three of us dug into that food as if we hadn't eaten in a month—and that's just about how I felt. Boy, I don't remember ever being so hungry in my whole life. And nothing ever tasted so good, either. There were a whole bunch of vegetable dishes with rice and noodles, and there were egg rolls and Chinese dumplings. "Hey," Simon said after we had finished a couple cartons, "they forgot the tea! I'm dying of thirst."

"Me too," I said. "Should I get us some water from the cooler?" I pointed across the room.

"Yeah, go on." He picked up the walkie-talkie and announced to the outside world: "Could you send us some tea? And those little cups."

I brought back three paper cups of water, and Simon put down his plate to take his. One thing he never put down was his gun.

When we first started eating—at his order, my ma dished up the plates while he watched over everything—we were all quiet, but in a while my ma and

I started talking. Just ordinary things, like about how good everything tasted and how much we liked Chinese food, and I said I missed the spareribs and pork. He just ate in silence, his cold green eyes darting between us and outside. But then he started to relax more, and in a while he was joining in and asking my ma how long she'd been a veggie; and before you knew it, the three of us were having a conversation almost the way friends do.

"Hey," he said, "you guys talk funny—where are you from?" When we told him, he got all interested and started asking us about New York. "Oh, man, I've always wanted to go there. Now maybe I'll have my chance. But I've got to wait for a while. Y'know, I just can't decide." He looked at my ma real seriously. "Where do you think the best place is to—you know—hide out? Till all this blows over."

"Well—well—" she began, and I could see she was pretty flabbergasted with that question. Suddenly there was a sound at the door, and we all looked over. A Chinese man in a white waiter's coat was holding a tray with a teapot and cups. One of the cops pushed the door open just far enough for him to set the tray down on the floor. When the door closed, Simon said, "Go get it, Danny."

"Ooh," my ma said when I brought it over, "almond cookies, my favorite!" There was a bowl full of them between the silver teapot and china cups.

"I personally prefer kumquats," Simon said.

My ma poured the tea, and we had it with the rest of the food. By the time we started opening the fortune cookies, she was looking a lot better, and I was feeling a lot better, too. This Simon wasn't such a bad guy, but his gun sure made me nervous. It was getting so it was hard to believe he'd really use it, but then you never knew. Every once in a while as we were talking in that friendly way he'd suddenly stop smiling and start looking serious, as if he was reminding himself not to get too chummy with people he might have to end up hurting. I wasn't even going to think of it as more than *hurting*. Not me.

Simon handed me the first fortune cookie. "Here, open this for me." I handed back the fortune, and he read it and burst out laughing: *"You will take a long trip."* That was the first time I saw him laugh. My ma and I opened the rest, and we all took turns reading them. They were the same old corny sayings you always get, until the last one, which Simon read: *"You will make a very successful business deal."* He slapped his thigh. "Darn right!" He paused, thinking hard. "What do you think of Crete?"

"I've never been there," my ma said, which made me realize it was a place.

"No," he went on, "I mean as somewhere for me to go to now. You know, till the heat dies down. It's supposed to be fantastic."

"I know," my ma said. "Are you Greek?"

"No."

"Can you speak Greek?"

He shook his head no. "Why?"

She shrugged. "Well, it seems to me you wouldn't want to go anywhere that you don't know the language. Not if you plan on staying for a while."

"Yeah, like that's a good point." He thought for a moment. "What about Acapulco? They must talk English there, so many Americans go there."

"I don't know," my ma told him, "I've never been there, either."

"Well," he said, "it's got to be a foreign country but—yeah, someplace where they talk English. Not England, it's too much like here. Oh, hey, I know—the Isle of Wight!"

"The Isle of *what?*" my ma asked.

"No, Wight. *That's* it! My grandmother—that spunky little old lady reminded me of her—she used to tell me about her rich English relatives, and some of them would go to the Isle of Wight for vacations. I remember the first time she told me I thought she was trying to say Right, but she'd go on and on about how she was there once when she was a little girl and how beautiful it was, and she'd take out the atlas and show me where it was, a tiny island off the coast of England somewhere. Then I heard about it again in that Beatle's song. When I was a little kid I always said that's where I was going when I got rich. Well"—and he reached for the walkie-talkie—"I'm rich."

For the next about hour or so, he was all business, talking back and forth with this special team they had set up to make a deal with him. The three of us sat there looking outside, Simon holding the walkie-talkie in one hand and that nasty little black thing in the other. He had started out by saying he wanted a plane to take him out of the country and enough money so he could live like a king. At first they didn't say much about it one way or the other. They just kept trying to talk him into giving us up and saying that then they'd see what they would do, but of course he nixed that.

"And when we make our deal," he told them, "I don't want any tricks. No FBI men or cops in disguise taking us out to that plane, or flying it."

Us, I thought. *Oh, brother!* I guess until that moment I kept thinking it would all be over any minute and we'd be rescued. Now I saw he really meant business. I got a desperate kind of feeling. That's when I knew I had to figure out something to save us.

Simon had the walkie-talkie on his lap, and he started tapping his foot nervously. "Man, what I need to soothe me is a little music. Yeah, *hey!*" He pressed the talk button. "Listen, could you send some music in here? Some nice mellow rock stuff—a radio or tape deck or something."

Right away they answered, "We'll work on it, Simon."

He laughed and rubbed the machine. "See that? It's a regular genie. I want something, all I do is ask for it. Yeah, hey, like that's a great idea, *music!*"

They sent in a tape deck with four cassettes of the pop songs you heard around a lot, and it was nice to hear music—sort of relaxing. You could see even Simon was easing up. Boy, I thought as I bent down to tie my shoelace, he wouldn't be so bad if he wasn't so crazy. Suddenly he swiveled, lowering his gun as he pointed it at me. I wouldn't have even noticed, but my ma's gasp made me look up.

"What're you doing?" he demanded.

I raised my palms. "Just tying my lace."

"Okay, but just don't try anything, y'hear?'

My hands were shaking so I could hardly tie the lace, but I made myself do it.

"Like this music?" he said to my ma now, as cool as could be, tapping his foot to the beat. She just smiled, and he nodded. "Me too."

Oh, brother! I thought again. And that's when I got my brainstorm. "Say, uh, Simon, there's a group from right around here I just heard the other night sounds like them. Even better."

"Yeah?" He looked at me with interest, even smiling a little. "What's their name?"

"The Four Brothers and a—Sister or a Mother, or something, I forget."

"Yeah?" says he again, then signals the cops, telling them: "How are the plans going? Listen, I want a plane and a hundred thousand dollars and a ride to the airport. I'm going to the Isle of Wight."

Of course they went through that Isle of *what?* business, and after he explained it all he went on: "No cops in disguise, no tricks. You don't harm me, I don't harm them. And just to make sure, I'm taking my hostages along." He smiled at us. "They might even want to stay."

I put my hand under my knee and crossed my fingers. "Hey, Simon," I said, "why don't you ask them to have a teenager drive us out to the airport? That way you'll be sure he won't be a cop or anything."

He nodded at me with a little smile. "Not a bad idea. A kid who just got his license."

"We'll line it up for you as fast as we can," they told him.

"Listen, while you're at it—there's a teenage rock group, The Four Brothers and a Sister or a Mother. I want them along—a personal appearance. Get a van, we'll have a nice mellow ride to the airport. Keep things calm."

My brainstorm had started working! If they came through—if the police could round them up—I knew my brothers could help us. I didn't want to go live on the Isle of Wight, not even if I lived like a king.

"It'll take some time," the cops were saying. "What did you say the name of that group is?"

Simon held the walkie-talkie in front of me, ordering: "Tell them, Danny."

I said, "The Four Brothers and a Mother— it's Chicky Fontina."

"And make it fast," Simon added. "I'm getting antsy."

"We'll do our best," they said.

I could see them scratching their heads. Then one of the cops from the sidelines came over to talk to them, and they all hurried back across the sidewalk to talk to some people we couldn't see. About ten minutes later they came back.

"Okay, Simon, it looks like we're going to be able to get you that group. It's a matter of rounding them all up, but we think we can do it. We have a van lined up, and the driver and the musicians are all teenagers. The plane is being checked and fueled at O'Hare and will be waiting for you with the money." He paused and said in this different, soft kind of voice: "Now Simon, won't you reconsider and let Laura and Danny Turner go when you leave here? We're complying with all your requests, and we give you our word—"

"No dice," he cut in. "I want to make sure this will go off right, for the first time in my life."

"You'll be just as safe without them, Simon, and it will be easier on you."

"No *sir*. I don't like to travel alone." He glanced over at us, his green gaze putting holes right through us. I was tempted to ask him to let us go, but I felt my ma's hard look. I could tell as I watched her, glancing back and forth between me and the gun, that she was warning me to keep quiet. It's so weird, but I could almost hear her thoughts.

"You guys," Simon said to us now, "keep on being smart the way you are, and you'll be okay. But don't be fooled. You won't be able to butter me up so you can manipulate me. After all, we're going to be spending a lot of time together, and let's be cool. I figured you for good company—my biorhythms told me you were the right ones, see? And like you're doing fine, so just stay mellow, and we won't have any trouble. But hey, I guarantee you guys, if you cross over the line—" He shrugged. "Well, I got too much at stake, that's all. Sometimes we have to make sacrifices in life. The love and peace thing, it didn't work for me. Nothing came my way. Hey, like I waited and waited, and I was real peaceful and loving. But everyone passed me by, everyone copped out, and I was left there all alone, see? Stranded. So now I figured like it's time for Simon to get his. But you always got to give up something to get something, if you want it bad enough, so—" He shrugged, pointing to his gun. "I gave up peace. And I'm sticking to it till the end, man." He let out a big yawn, then turned on the walkie-talkie. "How're we doing out there with the arrangements? Time's a-wastin'."

We sat around listening to those dumb tapes, but it was really good medicine for all of us, because it calmed Simon down like nobody's business. And when he relaxed it helped us feel a little better, too. Boy, I had never seen my ma so quiet in her life. I realized she must have him pretty much figured out and decided the best way to handle him was to go along real quiet the way she was. I could see her biting in her lip when I did that business about the Four Brothers and all; and I couldn't tell if she was glad or mad or scared or what, but I had this feeling inside me it was worth the gamble—that they'd figure out some way to help us get free. But now, as I watched Simon tapping his foot, I wondered if the cops really got the right guys, or if they just said they did, figuring Simon wouldn't know the difference.

The voice from outside came over the walkie-talkie. "Everything's shaping up for your departure. The van is on its way, the plane is being checked out, everything's going along. Now look, Simon, we have the money, the pilot is all set. Take Danny and Laura Turner to the plane if you must, but let them go once you board. You'll only make it more uncomfortable for yourself, having to keep an eye on them on that long trip."

"I don't want to hear any more about it!" he snapped. "I'm making the plans, and if you want to go along with them you can. If not, you have two lives here on the line."

I stared at him as if my look could blot out his words. There was this funny, hollow feeling in my head. Finally I moved my eyes and shook my head to get rid of that spookiness. And then I knew what it was. It was reality. The most awful truth in the world: our lives, my ma's and mine, that's what he was talking about. The realness of the whole thing hadn't reached me till that moment. Now that it had, I thought about all the fun and good times I'd had in my life, back in New York, and now here in Chicago. It was creepy to be thinking like that, but I couldn't help it. It was as if in those couple of minutes I had suddenly grown old. Right then I felt like my own grandfather.

"All right, Simon, relax. . . . What?" There was a pause. "Oh, I was just told the van is on its—here it is. Okay, Simon, we're all set for you out here. Are you ready to come out?"

"Yeah, man, we're ready to come out. Now, this is how I want it." He told them that the van should pull up to the curb right in front and that no one should be within a hundred feet of us as we left the bank and got into the van. They said all right, and Simon replied, "Okay, we're coming out."

He released the talk button and froze us with his icy gaze. "You're going to walk right in front of me," he told my ma, "just as close as we can get. I'm going to hold onto you, and Sonny is going to hold onto you, too. We're going to be real close, with my little friend right up there." I knew he meant his gun. "So behave yourselves, and we'll all do fine."

Before we even got to the door, I could see Tom's brother's blue van pulled up outside, just the way I knew it would be. I stole a look at my ma as I put my arm around her waist. She closed her eyes for just a second and moved her lips silently. Then I stared straight ahead. I could feel the warmth of both their bodies as we shuffled along. "Push the door open," Simon ordered, and we did. I had to blink at the bright sunshine, and looked around as much as I could without moving my head. I was amazed. The streets were crowded as far as you could see, and along the edge of the sidewalk were those wooden horses they use to keep back crowds. I heard the sound of cameras whirring, and wondered if we were on TV that very moment or if they were going to save it for the evening news.

Chapter 9

The old blue van stood at the curb with its front door open. Behind the wheel sat Tom with this funny look, trying to smile and not smile at the same time. I winked at him, and he gave the tiniest nod. I had no idea what my ma was doing, besides trembling, because I didn't dare turn my head. I felt like part of a three-piece organism, with those other two bodies so close to mine. It reminded me of how I felt when I was in a three-legged race in second grade, and I tried not to laugh. We took that high step up into the van, Simon bumping me with his knees; and there in the back were almost exactly who I expected: Chicky, chewing furiously on his gum, Lester, Julian, and—surprise: instead of Marcus, Bones stood by the drums. I didn't know Bones played drums; I figured they probably couldn't find Marcus. Now I noticed someone else in the back, and as I squinted to get my eyes used to the darkness, I made out Raymond! Well, listen, I can't tell you how I felt when I saw those guys. It was like a hundred-pound rock being lifted from my chest. I didn't see how they were going to be able to help us, but it sure felt good having them there.

Simon looked around at them pretty hard to make sure they were okay. It was real crowded there in the back of the van with all those guys and their instruments and the amp that they had plugged into the cigarette lighter. Just as I wondered what Raymond was supposed to be doing, Simon pointed at him and asked, "Who's that, the Mother?" They all laughed, but Raymond answered, "We couldn't get her so I'm filling in."

Aha, thought I, *so that's it! Leave it to Raymond not to be left out of anything!*

Simon nodded. He still had me and my ma huddled up against him. "That's cool. So now you're the Four Brothers and Another." Everyone laughed a little, and now he sat the three of us down in the seat behind Tom. "Let's go," he told him, and Tom put it into gear. Then, turning toward the musicians as Tom pulled away from the curb, Simon said, "Let's hear it. Something nice and mellow."

So there we were, bopping along in Tom's brother's beat-up old van to the live sounds of "Heartsong," with Raymond Frog Rafferty doing the vocals in a funny, hoarse voice that sounded really weird over the mike, and Simon humming along and tapping his foot. The music bounced off the walls of the van and made my head hum. If the whole thing hadn't been so scary, I would have had to laugh at Bones faking on the drums and Raymond faking on the lyrics. But the music did take some of that awful tension out of the air. I could see even my ma starting to relax a little; and Simon, keeping his steady watch with his gun propped on his knee, was helping out with the singing. Out the back window I could see some police following, but there was a lot of traffic, and everything looked normal. The song ended with a wild drum solo, and then the van sputtered, stalled, and stopped dead.

"What's wrong?" Simon yelled, springing up and over to Tom. Not till then did I realize the drum solo was really the sound of backfiring.

Tom was nervously working the ignition key. "I don't think it's the battery, it's turning over." It caught again, then sputtered and died.

"Try starting it again," Simon ordered tensely. Tom did, and the same thing happened. He looked up at Simon nervously. "Do you know much about cars?"

"Nope. Do you?"

"Not much." He turned to the musicians. "Hey, any of you guys know about cars?"

Raymond spoke up: "I do. It sounds like a radiator blockage to me. Want me to take a look at her?"

"Yeah," Simon said; and then, as Raymond headed for the door, "Hey, where you going?" He had his trusty little gun aimed right at him.

Raymond nodded at the door. "Out there to look at the radiator." He was real cool—he was great.

Simon, looking at the big hump in the middle

of the van, said, "I thought the works were in here."

"The motor," Tom said, "but the battery and radiator are out there under the hood."

Simon relaxed the gun and smiled sheepishly. "Oh, yeah, right."

"Want me to go out and take a look?" Raymond asked again, nice and steady. By now all the cars were going around us. We were in the right lane, next to an empty field of grass, rocks, and dirt.

"We'll have to get her pushed over," Simon said, looking out at the heavy traffic. "Hey, we're lucky, there's a nice open place right here. Come on, all of you, except—" and he nodded at me and my ma—"you two. You stay here, you don't weigh that much." He turned back to the guys, holding his gun up as he started out the door. "Okay, no funny business. I'll direct this operation."

Raymond, the last one out, was ordered to close the door, and then they all pushed the van over onto the field. My ma and I watched through the window as Tom and Raymond opened the hood and started looking inside while the other guys stood back where Simon told them.

"Hey, I think I see the problem!" Raymond cried. "Look!" Tom stuck his head in next to Raymond, who yelled, "Push that radiator cap down hard! Both of you, *real quick*—" Simon, shifting his gun to his left hand, reached over with his right, along with Tom, to where Raymond was pointing. In the very same moment, Bones leaped onto Simon from behind, pinning his right arm around Simon's neck in a stranglehold, while with his left hand, he twisted Simon's left wrist, instantly loosening his grip on the gun. It dropped to the ground, and Chicky sprang over and grabbed it. The police cars were pulling over now, their lights flashing; and the cops were pouring out of them with their guns drawn. The first one out rushed over to Chicky and took the gun from him. Chicky fainted. Bones released Simon, who had turned an awful color; and now we couldn't see him any more, he was all surrounded with cops.

The van door flew open, and a cop stuck his head in. "Laura, Danny, are you okay in there?"

"Wayne!" my ma screeched. We both started for him, and that's when my ma keeled over, right into his arms. Another cop's head poked in, and Wayne called, "Hey, Joe, get a medic in here, she fainted." Through the open doors I could see a whole tangle of squad cars, a police van, an ambulance, some unmarked police cars, and more vehicles pulling over. The drab little empty field looked like a parking lot where soon there wouldn't be any spaces. An ambulance attendant was bending over Chicky, and then I saw him sit up. I remember wondering if he choked on his chewing gum.

There were people all over the place. I could see some men unloading cameras and TV equipment from a van while others were already grinding away at theirs. And in the next moment it seemed like everyone was pouring into our van, led by the other ambulance attendant who rushed over to revive my ma.

As soon as she opened her eyes, she reached for me and gave me a weak hug. Wayne was bending over us, and it was as if he was trying to be all official as he said: "The danger's all over now, you can relax. Are you okay?"

My ma nodded. "Yes. But what happened to Simon?"

Wayne looked confused for a moment, then said, "Oh, the perpetrator! Don't worry about him, he's in custody."

My ma rushed for the door. "Wait—I have to see him!" She went flying outside, me after her, and got over to the police wagon just in time to see Simon's foot pulling in before the doors closed. "Wait, Officer, wait!" my ma cried, pounding on the door. A cop poked his head out, looking amazed. "Please," she said, "I'm the hostage. My boy and I, we just want to say good-by to Simon."

Now Simon's face appeared next to the officer's. His eyes, no longer bright and flashing, were dull and sort of glazed, and his voice was so low we had to strain to hear him: "Like, it isn't fair, man. Those fortune cookies lied."

My ma shook her head. "Not altogether. You're going on a trip, Simon."

"Yeah, ha. Very funny. Hey, I couldn't even make it as a bank robber."

My ma's face was real pale now, and her lips trembled as she said, "All that time there, you were holding that gun on me and Danny. Simon, you could have *killed* us."

"But I didn't," he said, "did I." The door closed on him, and now we were surrounded by a crowd that was growing bigger. Wayne had pushed his way through and was standing close. I spotted Raymond and Tom and started waving and yelling at them, and Wayne cleared a path for all the Brothers as they swooped down on us with shouts and whooping.

They had Bones up on their shoulders and were yelling, "He did it, he did it! He'll get the Purple Heart!" Wayne, laughing, reached up to shake Bones's hand. "He did it, too, you know," Wayne said, pointing at Tom, then at Raymond. "And him" pointing at Chicky, "and him, and all those guys. They were all part of it." He turned to me and my ma. "Did you think Tom's van broke down by accident?"

"Didn't it?" she asked.

I shook my head. "I should have known." But now I knew—that, and a whole lot of other things. Just like that feeling I had back there in the bank when I knew for real that our lives, my ma's and mine, were on the line. As I looked around at these guys—the ones who had adopted me as their kid brother for all different kinds of reasons—I suddenly understood that they had put their lives on the line for us, too. I wondered if they had stopped to think about the danger when they set out in that old van. And that was when I realized how far we had come together, me and my ma and my Big Brothers. They had helped me do a lot of growing up in a pretty short time. I had the feeling none of us would ever see the world in the same way after this.

By now they were all in a circle around me and my ma, and she was grabbing each of them and hugging and kissing them. Bones leaned down and lifted her partway off the ground, and the guys started picking me up and tossing me among them like a football. It was a pretty wild scene, and the happiest moment I had had in a lot of hours. Men and women started crowding in on us with their TV cameras and flashbulbs and microphones, asking a million questions from "How do you feel?" to "What happened?" I had to laugh at how all the Brothers were trying to tell the story at once. And what a story!

Raymond had found out about the bank holdup and the hostages and all, and had come down with Tom and Bones. Wayne, on duty, had been sent to the scene, and he had spotted Tom and Raymond. When Simon's demands came through, Wayne brought Tom and Raymond over to the hostage negotiating team and told them about Tom's brother's van and how they were friends of Chicky and his group. Wayne was sent with them to get the van and round up the band. Marcus was the only one they couldn't find, and that's when Bones got the idea of taking his place, saying he could fake it on the drums. Tom and Raymond figured out how to rig the van so it would run for about a quarter of a mile and then break down, by disconnecting the rubber hose to the fuel tank and plugging it with a pencil, and the police had planned to take over then.

But Bones had already plotted his part, telling the Brothers he was going to make his move but not to let the police know because they'd nix it.

"Which of you are brothers?" one of the reporters asked when the story was finished. My ma and Wayne and the guys and I, we all looked at each other and smiled, and then Tom and Bones said, "We all are."

Well, between all the different skin colors and styles of background, you can imagine the confusion. The questions were like spaghetti, all getting tangled and stuck together, and everyone trying to explain about me being their kid brother, and then my good old ma piping up, "It's all because Danny here wanted to become a Renaissance Man." They said "A *what?*" at which point she gasped and asked what time it was. "Four o'clock!" she cried, close to tears now as she turned to me. "Oh, Danny—we missed the show! After I paid so much money for those tickets!"

I shrugged. "Oh, well, Ma, we had a pretty good show of our own."

"Excuse me," a tall, thin, red-haired man said to my ma, "but I wanted to tell you how glad I am that you're all right. I'm Gus Jacoby."

"Thank you, Mr. Jac—oh, Mr. Jacoby! You're the agent I talked to the other week."

He smiled. "Yesterday."

She laughed. "Yes, but it seems like the other week. Well, isn't it nice that you're here."

"Yes, well—I heard about it over my car radio,

so I came over for a look. What a show!"

"See?" I said to her, and she laughed.

"Mrs. Turner, I can't tell you how glad I am that you and your boy are safe and sound!" chirped this familiar voice, and we turned to see the little white-haired woman from the bank.

"Oh, thank you!" my ma cried, hugging her; and now the other customers started crowding around and telling us how glad they were that we were safe. My ma suddenly got all crinkly-faced, and I was scared she was going to cry as she said, "I want you to know how grateful Danny and I are for your caring." She looked around, and everyone got quiet as she went on: "I can't believe that all this went on just to protect us!" She pulled me close. "It's—well, it's just overwhelming is what it is!" She bit her lip, and a tear slid down her cheek. Everyone started clapping. I bit my lip then, but it didn't help, either. I felt a tear slide down my cheek.

A man with curly hair and glasses came over. "Ms. Turner, I'm from the TV network. I have a message for you that Gretchen Andersen from our New York station is on her way out here to do a special program on the day's event from our studio tonight. She wanted you to know she's happy you and Danny are all right and hopes you will both make the evening available for her show." He glanced at the Brothers. "And those guys, too."

My ma's mouth dropped open, and I let out a whooping yell.

"We have just about all of it on film," he went

on. “Suppose we send a car for you at seven? I’ll make arrangements with the other boys.”

Gus Jacoby tapped my ma on the shoulder. “You won’t forget about setting up a date to sing for me, will you?” He grinned. “Now that you’re becoming a celebrity.”

My ma turned to Chicky, standing close by with all the other guys. “What about it—when can we perform for him?”

“How about now?” Julian said.

“Now—you mean right out here?” Lester asked.

“Why not?” Chicky agreed. “It’ll be fun!”

“Yeah,” Julian cried, “our own Woodstock!”

Chicky laughed. “Let’s give it a shot—we just about got warmed up in there!”

“It’s a great idea!” my ma cried. “But Chicky”—and she bent over to examine him, the way mothers do—“are you sure you’re up to it? Mmm, you’ve got your color back. Wow, now you’ve *really* got it back!”

We all laughed at his blushing. “Listen, I’m fine! I just stumbled back there when I went for the gun. I could do an hour concert right this minute. Are you sure *you’re* okay? You’re the one who fainted.”

She laughed happily. “I’ve never felt better in my life! Let’s go, fellas.”

Mr. Jacoby turned to Bones. “What do you say, Champ—can you fake it on drums again?”

The Brothers ran to the van for their instruments and equipment, and after Tom and Raymond reconnected the fuel line and checked out the van I helped them hook up the amp and the mike. Tom started the motor as they plugged in their instruments, and in the next magic moment that grubby field in downtown Chicago turned into an outdoor rock concert.

The first number was "Heartsong," this time with my ma on the vocals. There was a pretty big audience, let me tell you: everyone who was there through the whole drama of Simon's capture and all the passersby who could squeeze in. The TV people were filming it all, and the newspaper people were snapping pictures and taking notes. When I asked the TV man in charge what they were going to do with what they were filming now, he said probably use a little of it on Gretchen Andersen's show and maybe some on that night's newscast.

The guys sounded pretty wild. Man, they were really into it! With the amp turned way up, and Bones getting carried away like a maniac on those drums, I figured they could hear us in the next state. It wasn't their best music, but there sure was lots of good energy there. And my ma, she was fantastic.

I looked over at Mr. Jacoby, real proud. "Well, how do you like them?"

He was squinching up his eyes, looking sort of like he was in pain. "They're loud." Then, smiling quickly, he added, "But your mother's a talent, Danny. She's really got something. Let's listen."

A humongus traffic jam had built up as cars slowed down to watch and listen, lots of them pulling over and blocking the right lane. The cops who were still there rushed over to deal with it while Mr. Jacoby and I made our way through the crowd to the band.

"You were very good, Ms. Turner," he told my ma, his eyes sparkling as he grabbed her arm. "And under pretty tough conditions. Listen, I know some people who would like to hear you. In fact, my man on the West Coast—"

"The West Coast!" I yelled. "Does that mean Hollywood?"

He laughed. "Sure does, young man. The studio I'm connected with out there—"

"Oh, no!" I interrupted again. "We were just getting used to it here!" I looked at my ma and felt like bawling. "All the Brothers—our apartment—my school—"

She squeezed my shoulder. "Relax, Danny, we're not going anywhere. Not for a while, at least." Now she looked at Mr. Jacoby with one of her dazzling smiles. "It's true what Danny says, we were just getting used to it here." I gave a sigh of relief. "But," she went on then, "it wouldn't hurt to talk about it, would it?"

I rolled my eyes. "Oh, brother! Here we go again."